DARK COAST
Racer

Michael J.P. Whitmer

2026, TWB Press
www.twbpress.com

Dark Coast Racer
Copyright © 2026 by Michael J.P. Whitmer

Edited by Terry Wright

Cover Art by Michael J.P. Whitmer

ISBN: 978-1-967888-10-8

Chapter 1

Dark Coast Florida circa 1920

Johnny Smith strolled down a slummy Oldport side street, conflicted about what he had to do. He took the long way to Club X, giving him plenty of time to think. Beggars stumbled from their street corners and stoops, shrouded in rags and reeking worse than the rancid fish smell coming from the docks. They held out shaky palms for any charity. Johnny didn't have time nor a dime for the likes of those unfortunate souls.

"Beat it. I don't need your bad luck rubbing off on me." He waved them away, annoyed he had to divert his course, even a hair.

"See ya' when your luck runs out," Johnny heard one of the beggars utter from under his hood, then he sank back into the shadows. The bum had a lot of nerve. Johnny thought about reaching for his blade and going back to teach the bum a lesson by cutting out his tongue. But Johnny already had someone to kill tonight. And it would be a friend and member of his crew, Eli.

Michael J.P. Whitmer

He arrived at the gambling hall Club X, marked by the letter carved in black on the exterior of the building. It was a leaning three-story shack that connected and aligned farther down the street to more lousy structures. The building looked like it was one tropical storm away from blowing over. The entrance was a hole in the wall where the smell of tobacco and whiskey batted back the portside stench.

He was welcomed by an empty lobby boarded up and abandoned. A staircase led up to where the laughter and lights were coming from. Before ascending the stairs, he straightened his black suit and then used a hand to comb back his jet-black hair. At the top level was a drawer running into the wall of a billiard saloon. Johnny pulled out the drawer, dropped in some change, shoved the drawer back, and called "Whiskey, straight." Then he pulled out the drawer again and there was his drink.

Johnny drank the whiskey in one gulp and slammed the glass on the bar counter upside down. *No one drinks for free.* He knew the rules. His crystal-clear blue eyes scrutinized the prospects throughout the room. At a card table where six players sat, a snazzy dressed high-roller ended a game of poker with the winning hand. Three roulette games were available, their dealers standing at the ready. A beautiful blonde barmaid, moved around the room like a pedal floating in the breeze.

Rose.

He hated this life for her, but he couldn't show it or stare long. Johnny turned his gaze up to the balcony where Mr. X stood in his expensive suit and hat, his big-bearded face glowering as if unsatisfied with the profits or at Johnny being late to work...or both. They locked eyes. Mr. X motioned him upstairs and stepped away from the banister.

Johnny moved toward the back of the room where the stairs to the office were located. As he passed Rose, they shared a glance and a touch. "I'm going to get you out of here one day." He had said it to her before. He was saving money. After each job he put some cash away, but it wasn't adding up fast enough; that's why he had been stealing from Mr. X. He blamed the shortages on Eli, the biggest sucker of the crew and the obvious choice for a scapegoat. "I've got something for you."

Her eyes darted up as if to see if Mr. X was watching. He wasn't. "Careful, Johnny."

"I'll take my chances." He pulled a postcard out of his jacket pocket and slid it into Rose's hand. It read: *Remote Pines: Thoroughly exclusive living for the modern family.*

She looked at the image of a picture-perfect neighborhood with giant houses surrounding a pond. A happy couple and their child were waving from a front porch.

"That could be us," Johnny said.

She beamed at him. "You promise?"

He winked. "You know it, doll."

She smiled and stuffed the postcard in her apron then floated back toward the poker table.

His gaze lingered on her retreating figure, the grace, the sheer poetry in motion. She would be his one day, to live happily ever after in Remote Pines. His fluttering heart, suspended on hope for better days to come, came crashing down as reality cut the strings. In his line of work, hope was easily drowned in a flood of blood and tears, fleeting as the souls he'd sent to oblivion by the point of his blade. No. Their day in the sun was on the horizon...just a little longer...just a little farther...just up those stairs.

He ascended the steps to Mr. X's office and walked into the dimly lit room filled with cigar smoke. Heavier in the air was the fresh scent of death. At the center of the room, blood pooled from Eli's tied carcass hunched in a chair. Johnny's crew stood around the kill, all looking glad it wasn't any of them.

Mr. X lifted Eli's head by the hair to show a

pummeled and lifeless face. He had been tortured first. Johnny would have killed him fast. A swipe of his blade.

"You missed all the action," Mr. X said.

"Seems like the job got done." Johnny stepped out to the balcony to overlook the club. His gaze fell on Rose.

Mr. X stood beside him. "Eli said some interesting things before he died."

"What's that?" Johnny had a guess, but his attention had been drawn to the snazzy dressed high-roller cheering that he'd won another hand. His face seemed familiar now that Johnny was observing closer. The dealer glanced up at the balcony and signaled with a nod that the house was losing more money than it had on hand.

"He said you took the money." Mr. X chewed on his cigar. "You're too smart for that, I know." He blew smoke.

Johnny smirked on the outside but screamed on the inside, *"That goddamned Eli better not get me killed."* "A man will say anything if he thinks it'll keep him from dying. You notice the high-roller cleaning us out." Johnny nodded toward the poker table, hoping to change the subject.

"I noticed him earlier. Something's fishy."

"He looks familiar." Johnny thought hard. "He was in here a few nights ago. Bigshot, lost big, made a stink. We had to throw him out."

"Take your crew and show him out again. This time make sure he doesn't come back."

Johnny nodded and motioned for the crew to follow him. Looked like he would get to kill someone today, after all.

#

The spiffy gambler waited for the dealer to divvy out the cards, but when Johnny and his crew circled the table, he stopped mid-deal.

The gambler didn't show any fear. "Must be my fan club."

Johnny approached him from one side while two of his crew rounded the gambler's blind side. "Your fun is over, pal. For good this time."

"My luck's not run out yet. Can't say the same for yours." The gambler mule kicked Johnny in the stomach and dodged the clutches of his crewman by ducking under the poker table. He popped up next to the dealer then made a dash for the exit stairs.

"Grab him," Johnny croaked, gasping for air.

The dealer and the other gamblers froze, too scared to move.

Johnny had positioned two of his crew by the stairs, and they were wrestling with the gambler when Johnny caught up. Even outnumbered, the gambler was about to beat the odds against him.

"Drag him out back." Johnny punched the gambler in the mouth, which got him to quit fighting long enough to muscle him down the steps. At the bottom, the gambler smirked as if he still had a card up his sleeve.

Johnny pulled out his knife and flashed it in the gambler's face. "You won't be smiling when I'm done with you."

In the dimly lit alley that stunk of vomit and urine, four henchmen shoved the gambler against a brick wall. Hooded vagrants scattered into the shadows. Two crewmen held the gambler in place while the other two took turns punching him: a fist to the nose, another across the jaw, an elbow to the gut, and a knee to the groin. None of their blows knocked the smile off his face.

"That's enough," Johnny shouted.

The crewmen let him go and stepped back to catch their breath. They had already beaten Eli to death earlier.

Johnny got in the gambler's face. "Now I'm curious...were you not the one we threw out of here a few days ago? As big a loser as they come...caused a scene when you went broke?"

The gambler stared up at Johnny, bloodied and winded from the beating. "Yeah, that was me. Funny how you treat me the same...win or lose."

"We don't tolerate cheating around here."

"I wasn't cheating."

"A man's luck don't go good overnight. You were cheating." Johnny twirled the knife in his hand and then lunged forward with the blade and drove it into the gambler's chest.

Still, that smile, that smirk, like this was some kind of a sick joke. He had a few moments left before death would take him. "This..." the gambler managed to say with a grimace. "Will change your luck." He held up a shimmering coin.

Johnny plucked it from the gambler's palm.

The gambler's body fell limp and slipped off the blade, slid down the wall and hunched over dead, the smile still on his face.

Johnny examined the coin: pure gold it seemed, oddly circular, badly worn, and he could see in the dim alley lighting strange symbols on one side, a cross on the other. Spanish? A lucky coin? As he held it pinched between his thumb and index finger, it suddenly turned from gold to black, and a black wind swept around it, swirling like a storm at sea to suddenly turn back to gold that radiated heat waves like a desert mirage. Awestruck, his mind wrestled with thoughts of ungodly powers, black magic, evil lust—

"Hello, Johnny." The voice came from a shadow in the corner of his mind, from under a blanket over his consciousness. *"Very dark thoughts you have in*

here."

Johnny's heart lurched. *What the hell is going on?*

"*You and I are going to do great things.*"

Get out of my head.

"*All your dreams will come true.*"

Panic took hold. *I'm going mad!*

"*All you need to do is kill a few people.*"

Johnny dropped the bloody knife and the coin to grip his temples as if that would force the foreign voice from his mind. *Leave me alone.*

"*Just trust me. I can give you and Rose the life you have always wanted.*"

Rose, how do you know about her?

"*Kids, house, white-picket fence, dream automobile. It will all be yours.*"

The gambler was right. My luck really has changed.

"Hey, Johnny...you okay?" one of the crew asked.

Johnny gasped, realized he was standing stoic and staring stone-faced at the coin in his hand. He thought he had dropped it. And the bloody knife...

What do you want from me?

"*Kill your crew...and Mr. X.*"

Chapter 2

Dark Coast circa 1970s

A storm approached from the east; dark clouds gathered in the Florida twilight. Ralph didn't like the complication and hoped it wouldn't be an omen of what was to come. He pulled his 1970 Plymouth Barracuda into a truck stop where two hired guns waited for him. Bud, he had worked with before. Solid trigger man. The other guy with a scar across his cheek was new in town. He had the tortured look of a man fresh out of prison. Even before Ralph got out of the car, he heard the two men conversing.

The new guy had trust issues. "Who the hell is this guy supposed to be?"

"Scary, huh?"

"I can't see his face."

Bud huffed. "That's the Dark Coast Racer. He's a local legend."

Ralph got out of his ride, left it idling, and walked up to the two thugs. A normal person might have been intimidated by the looks of them:

weathered, scarred, long coats, collars upturned. However, Ralph wasn't normal by any measure.

"Hey, Racer." Bud welcomed him with a head nod.

The new guy offered a handshake. "Name's Marc. Put it there."

Ralph knew Marc could only see his own reflection in the visor of the black racing helmet he wore. "Evening, boys." He ignored Marc's hand.

Marc dropped his hand and scoffed. "So, you don't show your face or shake hands? Think you're too good for the likes of us?"

"Let's go." Ralph had a time schedule to keep. The Syndicate didn't like delays. And a storm was coming.

Ralph pivoted on his black boot heels and strode back to his idling hotrod. He could hear Bud and Marc grab two duffle bags. He didn't know what they were delivering, and he preferred it that way. The less he knew about the job, the better it was for him and his family.

He took his place behind the wheel. Bud and Marc slid into the back seat with the bags.

Ralph shifted out of park and hit the gas. The V8 hemi engine roared as the car tore out of the parking lot.

The sun had just fallen out of sight in the west, the last few rays of light shrinking, the night sky growing. To their left, the Atlantic Ocean heaved as the storm raged offshore. Flashes of lightning split the distant darkness. Farther down the highway, just past an orange grove, Ralph exited to a dirt road.

"Where the hell are we going?" Marc barked in the backseat, clutching one of the bags and an Uzi he had unholstered, as if anticipating trouble at the meeting point.

Bud kept silent, but he had his 9mm pistol in his lap and a look in his eyes that said life or death.

Ralph shut off the headlights as he steered the hotrod into a bend lined with oaks and pine trees covered with moss. The car was consumed by the darkness.

"Are you crazy?" Marc barked again.

Ralph trusted his instincts and the last image he had captured of the layout of the road going into the forest. He made only a few corrections to the wheel to keep on course. Breaking from the cover of the trees and driving into a vacant field, Ralph saw a truck's headlights in the distance.

"Look alive," Ralph uttered from under his helmet. Trust was fickle between the Syndicate factions. He could never be too careful when dealing with any of them. Turning the headlights on, he proceeded up the path toward the meeting point.

Two masked goons stood outside the truck, each with a black duffle bag in one hand and an assault rifle in the other.

Bud and Marc prepared to exit the ride.

"Leave the bags." Ralph reminded them both but meant it for Marc. "Confirm the cash first. Come back for the bags."

They nodded and left the bags on the seat.

Ralph watched the group meet in the cones of light from the headlights. As Bud and Marc peeked into the unzipped black duffle bags, a flash of lightning lit the sky and field, revealing three other parked vehicles on the perimeter of the meeting point.

"It's a trap," Ralph screamed out the window.

The vehicles in the distance kicked up dirt as their tires spun, propelling them to surround the group. Bangs and pops and muzzle flashes tore through the night as the two groups exchanged gunfire.

Ralph heard the door close, pressed the gas, and spun the wheel back toward the way they had come.

"Where's Bud?"

"He didn't make it," Marc yelled.

"It was a set up. Who would be crazy enough to cross the Syndicate?"

To answer his question red, white, and blue

lights flashed from the roofs of the vehicles pursuing them.

"It's the cops," Marc declared as if Ralph couldn't hear the sirens.

He shifted again, putting the hotrod in its top gear as he tore off the dirt road and back onto the highway. The flashing lights faded in the distance. After another exit and turn down a dirt road that was as narrow as a hiking trail, he parked behind a road sign and killed the lights.

Ralph glanced back to Marc to see he had managed to get away with both black bags from the drop off.

"Good spot to die." Marc pointed his Uzi at Ralph's head.

With a swift head movement, Ralph headbutted the gun barrel away with his helmet. He then shoved the driver seat back and squished Marc against the backseat. Spinning around, he reached over the seatback, grabbed the gun barrel, and twisted it toward the window. As Uzi fire shattered the window, Ralph beat Marc's face with his free fist. Marc was blinded by the first few blows. The next eight smashed his skull in and knocked him unconscious. The final punch killed him and left Marc's face a dented bloody mess. A cheek bone protruded from an eye socket.

Ralph let up the seat and resituated his helmet.

Blood and brain matter slid down the visor. He grabbed a blood-soaked black bag from Marc's lap and looked inside. White bricks.

"Cocaine!"

Chapter 3

It was after-hours at Gator's Tail Raceway when Ralph steered the Plymouth Barracuda through the back entrance gate and up to the garage. Gator was waiting for him at the open door. Gator was his handler and the closest person he had to a brother. Ralph parked and jumped out of the car, removed his helmet, and threw it across the shop and onto a nearby workbench.

"Damn it, Gator. It was a set up."

"I know." Gator rubbed his neck. "I got the call a few hours ago."

"What? The Syndicate called you?" Ralph glared at Gator.

His face turned pale.

"What did you tell them?" Ralph gripped Gator by the jacket lapels and drove him back to the workbench. "Did you tell them about me? About my family?"

"No. But I had to give them something."

"Don't tell me the Syndicate got to you." The reflection in the visor of his helmet on the workbench revealed multiple masked goons stepping from the shadowed spaces of the garage. He tightened his grip on Gator's jacket, wishing it was his throat. "What have you done?"

"They arrived just before you got here." Gator whispered the last part like he had done Ralph a favor while looking past him at the approaching assailants.

Ralph reached into Gator's jacket, pulled out his snub-nosed .38 Special, spun around, and shot two rounds into the nearest two goons. Bullets zinged through the garage as the other two goons squeezed their triggers. Ralph took a bullet to the shoulder, and another grazed his neck. His riding leathers provided minimal protection. Anger and adrenaline coursed through him. The need to survive to see his wife, son, and unborn child fueled his instinct to push past the pain.

Ralph aimed the pistol between the next goon's eyes and fired. The headshot dropped him instantly. As Ralph turned on the last goon and fired, he ducked two more bullets, that forced his aim off the mark. The rounds ripped past him, and one found flesh in Gator's leg, dropping him. To save his last bullet, Ralph flung the helmet. It hummed through the air and smashed into the goon's face, knocking him to the ground where he rolled in agony. Ralph stood over the goon and put the last bullet in his head.

"I'm sorry, Ralph." Gator stood with the support of the workbench, but he looked shaky and grimaced.

"Call an ambulance before you bleed out."

"What about you?" Gator nodded at Ralph's bleeding shoulder.

"Tell the Syndicate that if they want their shit back, they can have it. But I'm out. I'm disappearing after this. The Dark Coast Racer is no more." He picked up the helmet and fitted it back on.

"You know that won't be so easy, stepping away from the Syndicate."

"They better back off." Ralph slid into the hotrod and realized he still had a bloody mess named Marc in the back seat. "Shit." He got out, dragged the carcass from the car and added it to the pile of dead guys in the garage. "Good luck explaining these bozos to the cops."

Back in the car, as his adrenaline rush faded, he could barely grip the steering wheel. The pain felt like it had caught fire in his shoulder and was spreading through the rest of his body. He'd almost been killed twice tonight, and to top it off, he'd been betrayed by his closest friend.

He peeled out of Gator's, smoked tires as he careened the Barracuda onto the highway, then squealed to a stop at a red light. He punched the dashboard and screamed inside his helmet. Rage was all he had left. He had to calm down before getting home to Mary and his son, Ramon.

Keep it together, Ralph. For your family's sake.

#

Ralph didn't feel well, at all. Loss of blood from the gunshot wound made him woozy. He had managed to patch the shoulder himself at his safehouse where he kept the Plymouth. Cleaning up the bloody back seat hadn't helped either. He would need surgical intervention to remove the bullet but was thankful that the bone and joint had been spared.

When he arrived at home in the family Buick, the living room light was on, which meant Mary was still up. She had said it before: she couldn't sleep when he was out "Playing Racer," as she called it. As he pulled into the driveway, she flung open the door. Her pregnant belly's silhouette stood out against the midnight oil burning behind her.

He greeted her at the door with a bouquet of flowers he had just bought at 7-11. "For you."

Mary blushed, smiled, and hugged him before taking the flowers. "You're later than usual. You had me worried."

Ralph gritted his teeth as she rubbed his shoulder.

"You're in pain." She closed the door behind them.

He sprawled out onto the sofa, stared at the ceiling, and thought about all the lives he had taken tonight. *It was them or me.*

Mary arranged the flowers in a crystal vase. "Are you going to tell me what happened?"

She doesn't need to know all the gory details, but he couldn't lie to her about the fix he was in. "The job didn't go well tonight. Ran into some trouble that followed me back to Gator's."

"Is he alright?"

"He'll live." Ralph sat up and looked down at the vacuum-marked carpet. Mary was a good woman. She didn't deserve to be kept worrying night after night. He was almost done. He almost had enough saved to start his own garage and racing team to enter the circuit. It never seemed like enough... He felt Mary sit next to him. Her belly and his unborn child pressed against him with a needed embrace.

"I told Gator, I'm out. Told him to tell the Syndicate the Dark Coast Racer is retired."

Mary squeezed him happily. "That's a good thing."

He stared at her with uncertainty instead of his steadfast confident racer gaze. "It's not going to be easy. I've got something of theirs. Simply giving it back may not be the end of it."

"Dad?" Ramon, his ten-year-old son, stepped out of the hallway, rubbing sleep from his eyes.

"Hey, buddy."

He dashed to Ralph. Mary scooted over to let them share a hug. The pain in Ralph's shoulder seemed far away. "You should be asleep, buddy."

"I missed you, dad."

"Did you have a good day?"

"I helped you with your engine in the garage. Like you showed me."

"You did?" He glanced at Mary. "You let him in the garage while I wasn't there?"

She smirked, nodding. "I supervised while he tightened the manifold bolts."

"Good job, buddy. My little mechanic."

The phone rang on the kitchen counter.

"Who's calling at this hour?" Holding her belly, Mary pried herself off the couch and picked up the receiver. "Hello? Hi, Gator. Yes, he's here." Her expression turned worried as she held the phone out to Ralph.

Ralph left Ramon on the couch to take the phone. "What is it now, Gator?"

"They said okay, but they want their merchandise. They'll have their guy meet you at the same spot as tonight."

Ralph swallowed. *Too easy. Another set up?* But

if he didn't play it out, he'd never be free of the Syndicate. "Okay, but I swear, Gator—"

"You're good, Ralph, but be careful. I hear the guy they're sending in is a certified homicidal maniac."

"What the hell am I driving into, Gator?"

"Hopefully, your last ride for the Syndicate."

Ralph looked at his family. Since the Syndicate knew about him, they knew about them. The stakes were never higher. "I don't know what they've got on you, Gator, but this better be on the up and up or you're a dead man."

He hung up the phone.

Chapter 4

The next night, in the rundown industrial side of town, Ralph walked into his safehouse, an old warehouse he had rented out under an alias to hide his Dark Coast Racer alter ego. Right away his instincts screamed at him that something was not right in his shop. A missing picture. A misplaced screwdriver. A car door ajar; someone had sat in his ride. *Someone is in here with me.* He kept his cool, acted clueless, walked to his workbench without a care in the world. His racing leathers lay folded neatly on the bench. He began slipping on them over his clothes. Last, he plucked the helmet off the hook on the wall amidst an assortment of tools.

"Now we can begin." A cold and collected voice spoke from the shadows in the back of the warehouse.

Ralph turned to see a suited man step forward: spiffy jacket, spiffy tie, black gloves. Cold blue stare. He rolled a golden coin from finger to finger, a cheap party trick made to look menacing.

"I guess you're the Syndicate's Boogeyman." Ralph had heard the stories of this homicidal maniac passed among various triggermen.

"I prefer Assassin to Boogeyman. And you're the Dark Coast Racer. Even more infamous. I'm a fan. The tabloids make you out to be a superhero...well, are you? Can you fly like they say you can?"

"I'm guessing Gator told you where to find me."

"He did. Some friends are to die for, huh?"

"Easier said than done."

"But he didn't tell me about this." The Assassin pocketed the coin and held up the photo that normally hung from the pushpin on his workbench backboard.

"Leave them out of this." Rage bubbled up. He grabbed a heavy wrench from the bench and brandished it like a club.

"Don't worry, Dark Coast Racer. It's their stuff the Syndicate wants, and for you they have no more need." He released the photo to let it flutter to the floor.

A distraction Ralph couldn't ignore. His family going down...a subtle threat—

The assassin reached into his jacket and flung a throwing knife at Ralph's chest.

Ralph used his helmet to bat it away.

The Assassin dashed toward him with a wicked blade drawn. Ralph rushed to meet the advance, the heavy wrench poised for battle. He lowered his bad shoulder to barrel into him, but in a blur, the Assassin dodged the charge, and with two quick swipes, the blade sliced through his leathers and tore into Ralph's left thigh and calf. He had never seen anyone move so fast, like a ghost riding a bolt of black lightning. He staggered and pivoted, using his momentum to whirl the wrench around and knock the Assassin into next Tuesday, but the wrench met dead air, as the Assassin had flanked him with a sidestep.

This unleashed momentum sent him to the floor where he landed on his back and rolled onto his injured shoulder. The pain nearly blinded him, but he kept rolling toward the car in a desperate attempt to escape and live to fight another day.

The Assassin threw the knife into Ralph's right leg, which further slowed him down. Ralph managed to hurl the wrench mid-roll. It spun horizontally through the air toward the Assassin's head, but he easily ducked the brain-bashing tool. A concealed spring mechanism sounded in the Assassin's suit sleeve, revealing a wrist sword.

Ralph scrambled toward his hotrod, but the Assassin loomed above him. A sharp pain flared from his back as the sword penetrated muscle and bone. Ralph let out a scream but continued his desperate crawl to his car.

"You have a lot of fight in you. I'll give you that." The assassin laughed and speared him again, this time through a kidney, Ralph feared.

He reached up to the ajar driver door, swung it full open, grabbed the steering wheel, and pulled himself onto the seat. A twist of the ignition key cranked the powerful Hemi engine to life, even as his own life was bleeding out. He no longer had the strength to pull the shifter into gear.

The Assassin stalked up to open the driver's door, now armed with a gasoline can.

"What? Are? You?" Ralph demanded, his breath mere painful gasps.

"The last face you'll ever see." He doused Ralph and the car in gasoline, then left a rivulet as he walked backwards toward the exit.

Ralph, exhausted, tried to force his bloody hand to the shifter, but all he could do was floor the gas, filling the shop with the sheer power of his anger.

At the door, the Assassin lit a stick match and dropped it. "Enjoy your last ride, Dark Coast Racer." As the flames raced toward the car, he picked up the duffle bags that were in the back seat and walked away as if what he had done was nothing.

With a whoosh, fire erupted inside the car. Ralph's last bit of adrenaline forced his hand to the shifter. He slammed it into drive and floored the gas. The blazing hotrod took off, slammed through the warehouse wall, and barreled down the road before exploding into a rolling ball of fire that lit up the Florida night sky.

Chapter 5

Dark Coast circa 1980s

Gator's Tail Raceway was packed for another big race. In the back garage, Ramon worked on an engine that had been blown in a recent run. Gator hobbled in with a walking cane; its handle was the shape of a little alligator skull. "How's it looking? Can you get it to run again?" Gator looked over Ramon's shoulder as he bent under the hood.

"I'll get it running again, don't you worry about that, Mr. Gator."

"That's my boy. Just like your dad."

"Mr. Gator, I appreciate the compliment, but I'm not like my dad...until I can race."

Gator laughed proudly then hobbled to the workbench. Above the tools hung old tabloids and flyers from when the Dark Coast Racer beat a jet dragster, the Black Mamba. Another was a newspaper clipping from when the Racer had daringly escaped a police pursuit. The headline read: Dark Coast Racer Lives to Ride Again.

"In time, kid. You'll get your chance." His

smile sagged. "But you know how your mom feels about you racing."

"I'm almost twenty. I'm old enough to make my own decisions."

"You're right. Look at you. Six-six? You're bigger than your dad was. But still, let's get your mom's blessing first."

Gator hobbled out of the garage to where the crowd cheered, and the dragsters revved their engines.

"That went well." Isaac, a mechanic and Ramon's friend, popped up from behind the workbench where he was staying out of sight on purpose.

"Geeze, Isaac. You said you'd have my back. Pitch him 'his mom doesn't need to know' line. Thanks for nothing." Ramon turned away from the broken race car, annoyed. The engine block was busted when it threw a rod. "Now I still need to convince my mom to support my racing career."

"Invite me over for dinner. I'll talk to your mom. She won't be able to resist my charms."

"In your dreams." Ramon rolled his eyes and threw a balled-up oil rag at Isaac's face.

"Don't hate." Isaac threw the rag back but it fell short.

They both laughed.

"Come on. You know you're always invited for

dinner." Ramon patted him on the back.

#

Ramon walked in through the front door of his house with Isaac in tow. They could smell something delicious coming from the kitchen. Hints of garlic and basil.

Ramon stepped on some Barbies in a pink convertible car by the foyer. Rowin, his kid sister, was nowhere in sight.

"Dang it, Row. Pick up your toys, will ya?"

Ramon and Isaac took seats at the table. Mary came out of the kitchen with plates of spaghetti and meatballs with a side of garlic bread. A salad bowl with mixed greens and grape tomatoes was already set out on the dinner table.

"Hi, mom."

"Hi, Mrs. Murphy."

"Did you grease-monkeys wash up good?"

"Yes," they replied in unison.

She puffed on a cigarette pressed between a red-lipstick grin while she put the plates in front of them. "Go ahead and eat, boys. Row and I already ate." She coughed.

"Thanks, Mrs. Murphy." Isaac swirled pasta on his fork.

"Hey, mom," Ramon said before starting on his meal.

"Yes?" She stopped at the kitchen entrance and

looked back, still puffing her cigarette.

"I talked to Gator about racing."

"Oh, again." She winced.

"He said he won't let me drive until I get your blessing."

"Ramon, you know how I feel about it."

"Racing is in my blood." That was his mantra. He never spoke about his dad being the Dark Coast Racer, accept to Isaac who was sworn to secrecy.

"If you want my approval, you're not going to get it. Gator... Racing... All of it led to your father's death. I don't even like you working at Gator's."

"Mom, please."

"No." She turned and blew smoke.

Ramon pushed away from the table and shot to his feet. "Fine. I'm out."

Isaac didn't stop stuffing his face, only looked up from his plate with noodles slurping into his mouth.

"Nice charm you got there, buddy." Ramon scoffed at Isaac who had talked a big game earlier about charming her in defense of racing.

Ramon grabbed a slice of garlic bread, took a bite, and tossed it back on the plate. Munching on the bread, he stormed to the front door and slammed it behind him.

Outside, he glanced at his sister's bedroom window facing the front of the house. Row glared at him. She had their dad's fierce eyes. *Little sisters. What do they know?* She stuck her tongue out at him and ducked away. *Can't live with 'em. Can't kill 'em.* He stalked down the driveway and onto the sidewalk where he looked up at the stars.

Dad. Are you up there? Are you watching? Can you hear me? I know you understand how bad I want to race. He hoped to see a star shoot across the sky or some other divine sign. His fists clinched as he waited for an answer. He got nothing but more disappointment, like even the heavens didn't approve of him racing.

Down at the end of the road, headlights beamed on and a Hemi V-8 engine revved, startling him. The car slowly rumbled forward. Now he could see it was a two-door hardtop, all black paint job. Plymouth Barracuda. When the hotrod reached him, it stopped, and the passenger window rolled down. He stooped to see the driver and got the shock of his life. There was no one inside the car. Chills rifled through his body. "What the—"

Static from the car's radio stopped him from swearing.

Then: "Get in."

Ramon stumbled back and fought to breathe. "Who...how? Am I going crazy?"

"Come on, buddy. Get in."

It sounded like his dad's voice was coming

from the speakers. He had to be hallucinating...but curiosity made him ask, "Dad?"

"That's right. Now, let's go."

Ramon swallowed hard. "You've got to be kidding me."

"We don't have all night, son."

"Oh...my...God...Dad!" With a trembling hand, he reached for the door handle.

"Not there. The other side. Take the driver's seat." The driver door popped open, as if by a divine hand.

Shock gripped his throat, but belief in his dad propelled his feet around the car. There, he hesitated to get in, looked up at the house, the light burning in Row's vacant bedroom window. Isaac was in there, stuffing his face. His mother was smoking up a storm. No one would witness him getting into this phantom car. He was on his own, sure...but he was with his dad.

He slid into a vinyl bucket seat. That, the three-spoke steering wheel, and the floor shifter in the center console took him back to a time when true muscle cars ruled the road, a time before his time, could well have been the dinosaurs, but he could feel the nostalgia, the vibration of the 426 Hemi under the hood, much like the thunder in his chest. The interior was minimalist in design, not like any car he had ever seen. Especially the dashboard. Just a speedometer with no number markings. No other gauges. No dials for the radio but there was a channel selected on the frequency display. The numbers were his dad's date of death.

"What's going on?" He felt strange asking a car such a question, but somehow it was a manifestation of his dad, in spirit, no doubt, but undeniable.

"Grab the wheel. Together we're gonna take down the ones responsible for my death...and for so much more evil throughout the Dark Coast."

"You mean the Syndicate?" Ramon had heard the stories, just like everyone else. He and Isaac had seen the thugs around Gator's on the regular.

"That's right, son. Gator still works for the Syndicate."

"You can read my thoughts?"

"When you're inside the car, we are connected, quantumly."

"Okay. Let's go get 'em." Ramon reached for the steering wheel.

"Wait." His dad's voice stopped him just inches from gripping the wheel.

"What?"

"This is serious, Ramon. Once you take control of this car, you will be the Dark Coast Racer."

"Why didn't you say that from the start?" Ramon grinned and grabbed the wheel.

Electricity jolted his body from his fingers down to his toes. Like he had just taken a cold plunge, his nervous system felt shocked all at once. Crackling energy encircled his body, and black racing leathers materialized over his clothes. A black helmet with a mirror-like visor formed around his head.

"Whoa. This is epic."

"Welcome to my world, son."

He feathered the gas pedal. The Hemi responded with a lurch, like it was alive, a beast that had to run free. The power purring beneath his foot sent a wave of heat up his leg, through his chest, and down to his tingling fingers. He was in control of the most magnificent racing machine the world had ever seen.

"Easy, buddy."

"Right. I understand. This is no toy. But before we race off to battle the Syndicate, can I show you something?"

"The playground?"

"It's not the same anymore."

"Show me."

Ramon eased into the throttle and cruised around the block to what was left of the neighborhood playground. Time and neglect had exacted a toll on the swing set, now rusted and leaning with only three chains and no seats. The skeletal monkey bars sagged as if mourning the loss of children at play, their laughter and screams of joy. "We used to come here when I was a kid."

"I remember. What happened to this place?"

"Mom said the Syndicate embezzled money from the HOA. Drove our community into bankruptcy. You should see the pool, just a rank pit in the ground. It's worse off than I can explain. Like most of the Dark Coast, crime and corruption everywhere."

"Mary... your mom. I miss her."

"She's not been the same since you died, as if a big chunk of her heart died with you. Her nerves are shot. She smokes three packs a day. It's Row I worry about. I wish she could have known you and mom before our world got turned upside down. Life isn't fair."

"I wish I could have been there."

"You could have, but for the friends you kept."

"It's my cross to bear." Static sizzled then silence filled the car. Ramon felt just as guilty as his dad. He had his reasons for driving for the Syndicate, just a Ramon had his reasons for working for Gator. Both reasons had a lot to do with fast cars.

"Where do we start?"

"With Gator. Head to his raceway."

Chapter 6

The night sky was clear of clouds, making the stars and moon shine more radiant, and driving with the headlights off easier. Behind the wheel, Ramon felt unbeatable. The car seemed to sense his movements before he made them, which made controlling the beast easier and smoother. The traffic he encountered was nothing to hinder his progress. He weaved in and out of the lanes like a shadowy blur. One kid in the backseat with his face pressed against the window, managed to catch a glimpse of Ramon zip in front of their mini van. There was no chance of getting to top speed, but he wondered if the car had a cap. He waited for his dad's voice to answer, but nothing.

A drive that would have taken him thirty to forty-five minutes took him fifteen minutes. Ramon had made it to the road to Gator's Tail Raceway.

His dad's voice came back on the radio. "Park there."

Ramon parked in the event vendor lot, which afforded him a view to the shop's back garage door. It was closed. He shutdown the loping Hemi.

Closer to the building, heavy-duty SUVs were parked. Gator's ridiculously pimped-out Cadillac Deville had been pulled up near the garage door, not in its usual front row parking spot.

"Those SUVs belong to the Syndicate thugs I was telling you about."

"They've gotten overly bold after all these years...conducting business in plain sight."

"I don't see any activity, dad."

"You will. Stay sharp." The radio went to static and then fell silent.

Ramon gripped the wheel tightly, hopefully ready for anything, like being spotted by the goons, taking fire, or running for his life.

The garage door opened. Gator stood under it, holding a large duffle bag. Two goons opened the back hatch of an SUV, hauled out a storage crate so large it required both of them to carry it inside the shop. The effort was far from poetry in motion, more like two of the Three Stooges on steroids.

Suddenly Gator's voice spilled out the radio. "Damn it. Have you boys been drinking? You look like a couple monkeys trying to impregnate a football. I'm crippled and I could handle it better than you clowns."

"I got it," another voice filtered in, as a third goon rushed in to help the two-man crew carry the crate.

Ramon chuckled. "These dudes are a joke."

"Don't be so sure about that, buddy. These guys are dangerous. Time to throw a wrench in the works. Floor it."

"Where?"

"Let's see what they've got in the crate."

"Got it. Crate." Ramon cranked up the Hemi, yanked the car out of park, and floored the gas pedal. The quiet night erupted into high-octane chaos. He steered the fishtailing car toward Gator and the crate. The inertia plastered his body into the back of his seat.

The bad guys heard the throaty howl of the supernaturally charged engine. Gator and his crew looked his way and started to scramble. Ramon thought he was going to run them down, shocked that his dad would have him do such a thing. Even if they deserved it, he didn't want to murder them.

"Dad, are you sure?"

"Not yet."

"Dad. We're gonna kill them."

"Steady as you go, son."

"But—"

"Let me know when you can see the whites of their eyes?"

"Dad. I can see their fricken pimples."

"Turn the wheel, hard left." His dad's voice commanded at the last second.

Ramon sent the car into a screeching three-sixty spin.

The three goons dived out of the way.

Gator dropped the duffle bag and fell to his knees, and then crossed his arms in front of his body as if bracing for what he thought was his last moment.

The spin ended when the bumper smashed into the crate. A white cloud of cocaine exploded into the air.

The driver's door flung itself open and knocked Gator in the face. He fell over.

Ramon noticed Gator had pissed his pants.

"Grab the bag," dad's voice told him.

Ramon leaned from the car, grabbed the duffle bag strap, and just as he sat upright, the door closed on its own. He smashed the gas pedal; the hotrod spun its tires and took off, leaving Gator covered in dust, cocaine, piss, and clutching a bloody nose.

"Get after 'em, damn it." Gator's voice still came through the radio.

Ramon watched in the rearview mirror as Gator flailed his arms, signaling his crew to go. The goons piled into the SUVs. One goon ran into the garage and then drove out in a fire-breathing dragster.

"Let's see what you got, son. Lose them."

"On it."

I could use some driving tunes, though.

Kickstart My Heart by Motley Crue blared from the speakers. Ramon smirked and gave the dash a loving pat as the car careened out of the parking lot and skidded back onto the main road.

"When I get high, I get high on speed." Ramon sang along as the dragster bore down on his rear bumper. The Barracuda surged forward, even with the gas pedal mashed to the floor. Yep. The supernatural turbocharge had a mind of its own.

The hotrod pulled away, leaving the dragster trailing and the SUVs lagging even farther behind.

"My heart, my heart, kickstart my heart."

Gunfire rattled behind him. Bullets pinged off the car, echoing through the interior in a sonata of impending total destruction. A jolt of fear knocked him for a loop. For the first time he thought he wouldn't make it out alive.

"The car's bulletproof," Dad said over the notes of a guitar riff. "Now we take the fight to them."

Ramon felt hot adrenaline hit his bloodstream, and he spun the wheel like he had a death wish. The car drifted before it grabbed traction and swung one hundred-eighty degrees and stopped, facing the dragster and three SUVs approaching as if they were flying in formation. His foot was on the brake, but the car took off like a bat out of hell, aiming straight for the bad guys. He guessed the speed had instantly jumped to a hundred miles an hour.

Machine-gun fire bounced off the windshield, spiderwebbing the glass, but the car wouldn't back down or detour from its charge. He was on a head-on collision course with the dragster.

"Dad?"

"Kickstart my heart, give it a start... Whoa, yeah, b-b-b-b-baby."

"Dad!"

The dragster swerved left so violently the driver lost control. The rear end clipped the SUV on the left, and they both careened into a wild spin. The SUV flipped. Its bulky frame rolled and tumbled down the road in a splay of torn metal, shattered glass, and loosed debris. The spinning dragster took out the SUV on the right. It flew off the road to crash somewhere in the darkness. The dragster didn't fly; it hit the guardrail with an angry grind. The third SUV driver hit the brakes, but his fate was in God's hands now. It slammed into the flipped SUV and ploughed both vehicles into the median's concrete retaining wall. Sparks flew. Spilled fuel ignited. The road became an inferno. The Barracuda executed an single-point U-turn and blasted through the wall of flames, leaving a vortex of swirling fire in its wake as it disappeared into the night.

The *Kickstart* song ended just as the chaos died.

Ramon felt like Han Solo piloting the Millennium Falcon away from the Death Star. The force was with him: 426 cubic inches of Hemi hellfire. To his amazement, the cracked windshield repaired itself, as did all the bullet knicks and dings.

"Good job, son."

"Me? This car is crazy."

Dad laughed. "We're not done yet, buddy. Find a safehouse to stash the car and money."

Ramon glanced at the duffle bag on the passenger seat. Syndicate money. Blood money. Nothing good could come of keeping it. "I know a spot, but I'm going to need a friend's help."

"Keep this close to your chest, buddy. The fewer who know, the more will live through the war that's coming."

Ramon steered the hotrod Plymouth down the dark highway. The helmet seemed suddenly too tight, the leathers creaky and unyielding. So far as he knew, no one had died tonight, but even so, he was a race car driver, at last. The Dark Coast Racer.

Radio static crackled.

"I'm on the highway to hell!"

"Dad! That's not funny."

Chapter 7

Isaac's bedside phone rarely rang, especially at 2:00 in the morning. He rolled over and fought with his covers to unravel himself and grab the receiver. "Hello?"

"Issac, I need your help."

"Ramon? Why do you sound like Batman?"

"Batman?"

"Your mom and sister are worried about you. Where did you go?"

"Did you hear me? I need your help, man."

"Yeah. I heard you. What's up?"

"I need you to pick me up in the old warehouse district. The building we found for our future auto repair shop."

"My dad'll kill me if I take the truck out at this time of night."

"You remember that time in eighth grade when you needed me to switch pants with you because you pissed yours, and you were suppose to meet Cindy after gym?"

"When will you let me live that one down?"

"Never. See you soon." Ramon hung up.

Speaking of pants. Where did I put mine? Dirty hamper or under the bed? Isaac rolled out of bed.

\#

Thirty minutes later, Isaac drove into the rundown industrial district where an explosion many years ago had driven out most of the businesses. He and Ramon had big dreams for the area. Once they built their car shop here, other businesses would follow. Only a few street lights were operable, so deep shadows surrounded much of the deserted compound. He wondered why Ramon wanted to meet him here.

He parked in front of the warehouse unit they were buying, left the truck running and the headlights on while he unlocked the padlock securing the garage door entrance. When he lifted the door up, he heard a 426 Hemi rumble to life behind him. He froze. The engine sounded different than most, mean-tempered. It growled as it loped at idle. He turned around to see an all-black Barracuda slowly lumber from the shadows. The throttle barked and the car lurched like a leashed Rottweiler.

The hairs on the back of his scalp tingled.

"We're closed," he shouted.

As the car approached, he stumbled backwards into the shop. The hotrod maneuvered past his truck and into the dark garage, blowing dust like a snorting beast. The thunder of internal combustion shook the walls.

Isaac inched deeper into the shadows. Curiosity dampened his instinct to run.

The muscle car was but a creeping silhouette against the sparse lighting outside. It stopped. The engine shut off. Sudden quiet filled the shop.

Isaac held his breath.

The driver door swung open, and a man stepped out, clad in all-black racing leathers and a matching full-face helmet with a visor that reflected glints of distant streetlight.

"What do you want?" Isaac demanded.

The driver walked directly to the switchbox and turned on the wall-mounted fluorescents.

In the settling dust, an incredible scene came to light, the blacked-out 1970 Barracuda, crouched like a sleeping panther, the masked driver walking toward him, a phantom-traveler from another world, it seemed.

"My friend's going to be here any minute. You better get out of here."

In one smooth motion, the driver took off his helmet. "Relax, Isaac."

Isaac didn't know whether to blink or go blind. He should have been relieved it was Ramon, but the adrenaline overload still had him grappling with fear. The car...the getup...the entrance straight out of a horror movie. "You son of a...you scared the crap out of me."

"Thanks for coming."

"Where in the hell did you get this car?"

"It's my dad's."

"The Dark Coast Racer? His car went up in smoke and ash. Nothing left of it."

"It's the same car."

Isaac circled the car and took in every curve and detail. His fingers caressed the black metal. "Nah. Somehow you found the spare time and money to restore an old Cuda."

"I didn't."

"Then how did you get it?"

"It came to me."

"What does that mean?" Isaac finished walking around the car and stopped at the hood. "You saying it's a zombie car?"

"I don't know what it is, but I've never seen anything like it."

"Let's pop the hood, get the engine serial number. That'll tell us where it came from." Isaac bent over and groped for the release lever.

"No," a voice shouted from inside the car.

Isaac straightened and glared at Ramon, brows furrowed.

"Who's with you?"

"That would be the ghost of my dad. He

speaks through the radio."

"Are you for real, man?" Isaac stepped to the passenger door; it wouldn't open. He shaded the tinted window with a hand but couldn't see inside. "Ralph. Is that you?"

"Never open the hood."

Isaac stalked back to Ramon. "Alright. Maybe you've got something here. Are you going to race his car on the circuit?"

"I'm not so sure that'll ever happen. I already asked. Dad's car is here strictly for revenge."

Isaac could barely think straight. "The Syndicate?"

"Wait 'til you see this." Ramon opened the passenger door, took the duffle bag off the seat, and tossed it on the floor at Isaac's feet. "Syndicate cash."

Isaac stepped back. "Oh, no, Ramon. They'll come looking for it."

"Exactly the point."

"So what do you need my help with?"

"I need to use this place to hide the Cuda and the cash." Ramon picked up the duffle bag. "There's more than enough here to build our shop and finance my racing plans."

Isaac gasped. "If the Syndicate doesn't kill us first, your mom sure as hell will."

Chapter 8

Ramon woke up in his bed. His kid sister stood over him, brushing her teeth. Morning light peeked through his window blinds.

"Where were you last night?" Rowin asked mid brushing, her words muffled as toothpaste bubbled out the sides of her mouth.

"Nunya business. Now, out of my room before you drip Crest all over the place." Ramon moaned, rolled back onto his side, and pulled the covers over his head. His mind was racing with all the action from last night; he wished it was a dream. *It'd be easier that way.* The waking world was complicated enough without adding drug money and a vigilante plot to avenge his father. *I could use another hour of sleep to escape the creeping thought of 'be careful what you wish for.'*

"Mr. Gator is here, talking with mom. You're probably fired." Rowin exited the room, still brushing her teeth.

Ramon shot up in bed at Gator's name. *Shit, he knows*. Ramon scrambled from under the covers, jumped off the bed, and dashed out of his room.

There's no way.

He thought about army-crawling on his belly through the hallway, but that seemed too dramatic. Instead, he stepped over the board in the floor that made a creak every time he walked on it. Stopping out of sight just at the end of the hallway where the dining room and living room met, he heard his mom and Gator talking at the dinner table. Cigarette smoke filled the room.

"He was here all night, Gator," his mom lied.

"Mary, I'm sorry. I hate to even question him. Ramon is a fine young man, but that was Ralph's car, for sure. There's no mistaking it. The driver cost the Syndicate a lot of money." Gator slurped coffee.

"My husband's car was burnt to ash, and I don't care about the Syndicate. We want no part of them."

"Mary, it's too late to play keep-away. If I don't get that money back, the Syndicate will go after anyone connected to the Dark Coast Racer... unless...you come with me, Mary. I can protect you."

"Thanks, but no thanks. I'll always be Ralph's girl, Gator. No scare tactics are going to change that."

"Damn it, Mary. I'm serious. Once I leave town, you'll be on your own."

"I've been on my own for fifteen years."

A knock at the front door interrupted the conversation. Ramon took the distraction as his chance to enter the room. "Morning, mom." Ramon faked a yawn and looked at Gator, acting surprised to see him. "Oh, hey, Mr. Gator. What happened to your nose?" It was bandaged up.

His mom and Gator got quiet while puffing their cigarettes and drinking coffee.

The knock sounded again, and Ramon answered the door.

"Is Row ready?" The neighborhood boy from across the street, Jeremy, was there to walk his sister to the school bus stop, as usual.

"One second." He half closed the door and yelled back into the house. "Hey, Row. Your boyfriend is here."

Row rushed from out of the hallway with her Power Rangers backpack hanging on by one shoulder strap. "He's not my boyfriend, dope." Her cheeks were red with embarrassment. "Bye, mom. Love you." She shoved past Ramon, giving him an elbow to his side. "Bye, jerk." She slammed the door.

Ramon turned back to the dinner table.

Gator had gotten up and was walking toward him with the aid of his cane.

"That nose looks pretty bad, Mr. Gator."

He limped up to him and put a hand on his

shoulder.

"An accident." He gestured to his nose like it was nothing. "See you tonight at the big race?"

"You bet."

Gator smiled, showing his gold tooth, looked back at Ramon's mom, and gestured with a farewell head-nod like it was his last goodbye. He left out the front door.

And maybe it is Gator's last goodbye. The Dark Coast Racer is back.

As soon as the door shut, his mom spoke up. "Where the hell were you last night?"

Shit. Ramon deflated a bit; he hadn't come up with a good excuse yet. "It's private."

"As long as you live under my roof nothing is private. Now tell me where you went last night."

"I...was with my girlfriend, mom. Can't a guy have any privacy?" He didn't feel good about lying to his mom. Superheroes had to lie to hide their identities from their loved ones. To keep them safe. *It was already dangerous enough looping in Isaac.*

"A girlfriend? Oh, that's good. Hopefully she'll get your mind off racing." She said it with a tone of relief as she got up from the table to clear the coffee mugs.

Ramon was still stuck on why Gator was here. He suspected him of being the driver last night? *No way he had figured that out.* "What did Gator want?"

"Gator was going on about how a guy driving your father's race car robbed him last night."

"That's impossible, mom."

"There's only one car like it. Insisted it couldn't have been a replica."

Ramon stayed silent by the door as she finished her cigarette then snuffed it out in an ashtray on the kitchen counter.

"Or he saw a ghost. Crazy, I know. Gator always held a torch for me. Jealous I loved your dad and not him. I never thought he'd come up with a ghost story to get me to run off with him."

"Mom, after tonight's race. I'm not going to work for Gator anymore."

"That's nice dear," she said only half listening and busy lighting up another cigarette.

I'm going fulltime Dark Coast Racer.

Chapter 9

Ramon couldn't get his mind off the Dark Coast Cuda and the money stashed at the warehouse. He stared blankly at the race cars, thinking of what his dad wanted him to do with the car's power versus what he wanted, which was to race. Now that he was at Gator's Tail Raceway, the urge to race weighed on him. As did the vibrations of the crowd cheering at dragster engines being revved and tire burnouts throwing smoke.

"Ramon, snap out of it." Isaac slapped him on the shoulder.

Ramon realized he had been holding the same lug nut for a few minutes. They were working on Gator's Cadillac, tuning it up for a road trip. He didn't say where to or for how long, but Ramon figured he was running from the Syndicate.

"I just wish I could race tonight."

"Keep dreaming, ass-wipe." A familiar voice chimed snidely from behind them.

Ramon and Isaac spun around to see Chase.

Isaac snorted. "Don't you have a race to get ready to lose, Chase?"

"It won't be him beating me, that's for sure." Chase pointed to Ramon.

"He's beaten you at everything from foot races to pie-eating contests."

"But he's no race car driver."

"Don't press your luck."

Ramon crossed his arms and leaned against the fender of the Cadillac, smiling smugly. He had driven the fastest race car on earth.

"Isaac, you're nothing but his cheerleader," Chase fired back. "He hasn't won anything when it counted."

The lug nut in Ramon's fist had more brains than Chase. "Scram, Chase." Ramon unfolded his arms and flipped the lug nut like tossing a coin. "We're working on Mr. Gator's ride. We don't have time for your dumbass." His cheeks felt red-hot with anger.

"Your mommy still won't let you race with the big boys." Chase chuckled. "You're a loser, Ramon." He turned on his heels, kicked a wrench on the floor, and walked out.

Ramon lunged at Chase, but Isaac stopped him with an arm across his chest. "He's not worth it, Ramon. He's a blowhard and a bully. He'll get his comeuppance someday." Then Isaac leaned in close to Ramon's shoulder and whispered, "Here, take my keys to the truck. Go get the Cuda and smoke this asshole, once and for all."

Ramon liked the idea, but: "I can't. Dad won't let me race the car."

"Come on, Ramon. I think your dad will understand." Isaac had said it like when they were kids asking for a sleepover on a school night. "Racing is in your blood, man. Just like your dad."

"Maybe..." *What's one race?* They could still complete their mission to destroy the Syndicate. Gator's already running scared, and revealing the Dark Coast Racer to the public could drive the Syndicate underground, afraid to show their faces. He took the keys from Isaac. "Alright, see you in a jiffy." Ramon was sure that his dad was not going to go for him racing the Cuda, blood or no blood. *But it's worth a shot to humiliate Chase.*

"You have an hour."

#

Ramon used the key to unlock the garage door. The Cuda's headlights beamed on as if welcoming him inside. "I see you can sense my presence."

"Yes." His dad's voice came from the radio.

"Can you drive without me?" *Who's really in control?* Ramon wanted to ask as he walked up to the Cuda.

"My ability to drive is limited now that you're the Racer."

After Ramon rounded the car, he entered the

driver side, and the motor turned on. The helmet lay on the passenger seat. "We've got Gator on the run. He's preparing for a trip with some of his crew."

"That's good news. The Syndicate won't let him get far...but why do I sense something heavy on your heart?"

"I want to drive your car in the race tonight."

"Absolutely not. It's too risky."

He clenched a fist. "I need to race, dad. I thought you'd understand."

"We have a mission."

"You have a mission. I want to race."

"The Syndicate has to be stopped before more people die."

"Is that the only reason you came back?"

"Yes. Get in. Get out. A clean operation."

"If you were alive you'd let me race."

"But I'm not alive. My time here is limited. The afterlife is not flexible when it comes to wasting that time."

"You want my help with your mission...I want to be in the driver's seat tonight. Fair is fair." Ramon grabbed the helmet and slid it over his head. The Dark Coast Racer leathers materialized over his body.

The engine revved up. "Let's go get 'em, son."

Chapter 10

Isaac paced nervously along the fence that separated the racetrack and the mechanic's garage. He wasn't far from the bleachers, rowdy with the fans. He drank the last of the Mountain Dew, crushed the can, and tossed it in the overflowing dumpster near the fence. His favorite soft drink added to his buzz of excitement. Over the track's loudspeakers, he heard the first pair of racers called to the starting line. *"Ladies and gentlemen. First up, number 92, State Champion Chase Mendez in his souped up Camaro Z-28, and his challenger, Rodney "Rocket" Rogers, number double-0 7, driving a Road Runner R/T/S. Are you ready for this, folks?"*

Isaac was about to have a fit. *Ramon's not going to make it. It was a longshot entering the race last minute with the Cuda. No vehicle inspection. No driver check. No equipment check. Plus, the whole dad's-voice-in-the-radio-of a-ghost-car was too much like something out of a Twilight Zone episode.*

"Isaac, where's Ramon?" Gator spoke from behind him, snapping him out of his thoughts. He nearly jumped out of his coveralls. He turned to see

Gator standing at the entrance to the garage and leaning on his gator-skull cane.

Isaac thought to stall him. "Ramon who?"

"The only Ramon that works here. Your damn best friend."

"Oh, that Ramon. I think he's in the crapper."

"I was just in there, taking a piss. He wasn't there."

"Oh, uh...the concessions maybe?"

"Is my Caddy ready?"

Isaac noticed luggage by the trunk of the Cadillac and two of Gator's goons in trench coats on standby. Wherever Gator was going, it looked like he'd be gone for a while. Odd for him to take off during the big race, though.

The dragster engines revved to ear splitting levels, then exploded when the green light flashed. As the dragsters tore down the track, there came another crash of thunder, distinctly more energized, that rose over the dragsters' roaring engines. The sound made Gator's face turn white.

It was the Dark Coast Racer.

Isaac turned to see the Cuda blur by and smash through the dumpster and fence. Trash and debris flew as he rocketed onto the track and blasted across the starting line. Red taillights left an afterglow in the racer's wake.

Chase and Rodney were neck-and-neck

halfway down the track. The Dark Coast Racer caught up with them, split the lanes, and tore past them to cross the finish line. The dragster drivers deployed their parachutes, but the Dark Coast Racer kept going. He crashed through the fence at the far end of the track, went off-road and faded into the Florida wilderness.

The fans hooted and hollered.

"Well, folks," came over the loudspeakers. *"What a turn of events. An unknown racer just blasted the doors off our two top competitors. Boy was that something. Who was that mysterious racer?"*

Isaac pumped his fist in the air. "Ramon, you did it. Holy shit."

"What? The son of a bitch!" Gator shouted. "I knew Ramon was behind the wheel of that damn car. Boys, grab Isaac's happy ass."

Shit! Isaac stiffened and felt his neck hairs prickle. He didn't mean to cheer out loud. The goons in the trench coats were fast, for big guys, and closed the distance to him before he could make a run for it. They tackled him easily; one got him in a rear chokehold. He tried to shout, "take your stinking paws off me, you damn dirty apes," but all that left his lips were choking murmurs before darkness smothered him.

#

Three hours later, Ramon eased the Cuda into

the nearly empty parking lot of Gator's Tail Raceway. The adrenaline rush still gripped his body. He had waited long enough to give the crowd time to clear out. Gator's Cadillac was idling inside the open garage door with its headlights on.

Ramon figured Gator would have been long gone by now.

"Careful, son." Dad spoke through the radio. "I sense something is off."

The Cadillac's brake lights flashed, the reverse lights came on, and the car backed out of the garage, wheeled around and headed for the main gate.

"See, nothing to worry about, dad. Come on. I bet Isaac is waiting." Ramon drove the Cuda toward the open garage door. As he neared, he maneuvered to take the spot where the Cadillac had been parked. He had a clear view of the garage interior. As if nightmares could rise from sleep, Isaac was tied to a chair in the center of the first bay; his head hung low, his coveralls bloodied. Behind him stood two trench-coat-clad goons, and Gator.

Ramon's eyes went wide. The devil himself...the betrayer of friends, had set a trap, and damned if he hadn't taken the bait and fallen right into it. "Dad?"

Gator waved at the car, grinning. His gold tooth flashed in the Cuda's headlights. "Get your ass over here, Ramon. I want my money." He jabbed his cane in the air.

"What do we do, dad?"

The Cadillac drove up behind the Cuda, boxing the car in the garage.

"Looks like we've got 'em right where we want 'em, son."

"Nowhere to go," Gator yelled. "What's it going to be? The money, or should we be beat on your buddy to death?"

One of the trench-coat-clad goons lifted Isaac's head by the hair and punched him in the face, adding to the bloody mess.

"Screw you," Isaac muttered defiantly and spit blood at his assailant.

To Ramon, that was the upside to this situation. Isaac still had some spunk left in him. Ramon grabbed the door handle.

"Wait," Dad said. "Let 'em sweat."

The Cuda's idling lope echoed through the garage.

"Fine." Gator motioned to the driver in the Cadillac. "Chase, drag his ass out of the car."

Ramon looked in his rearview mirror to see the Cadillac driver's door open. Chase stumbled out clutching his neck with both hands. Blood spewed between his fingers from a slash across his throat. He didn't shout or scream as he staggered forward and collapsed onto the pavement.

By the horrific expression on Gator's face, and the fact his goons took two steps back from Isaac, they appeared just as stunned as Ramon.

"Something else is going on here, Dad."

Gator sent one of the goons to investigate.

Ramon watched him draw his Glock and close in on Chase's body, now lying motionless in a pool of blood. He kneeled to Chase, but not too close. "He's dead for sure, boss. Why would he cut his own throat?"

Yeah. Chase was a jerk, but he didn't deserve that. Ramon felt sorry for him, even as a new sense of dread swelled in his gut. "Dad? What's going on here?"

"Shit's gonna hit the fan, buddy."

The passenger door to the Cadillac swung open. A shadowy figure stepped out. A dark mist swirled through the air, filling the garage with an ethereal haze.

Gator backed away, trembling in sheer terror, his face suddenly ashen, his wide eyes filled with recognition. His mouth hung open as if he wanted to scream.

"It's him," his dad said, quiet as a whisper in church.

"Who?"

"The Assassin."

Ramon could see him in the rearview mirror. "He looks like the grim reaper."

"You're looking at pure evil, son, the demon that killed me."

"Demon?"

"See how the shadows move for him. That mist is his breath, from deep in his dead lungs. The perfect killing machine, the left hand of the devil, the right hand of the Syndicate. Whatever you do, don't get out of the car. I can't protect you out there."

Gator jumped behind Isaac and stooped low as he could go. "Kill him, boys."

The goon outside the garage, kneeling to Chase, popped up and opened fire at the shadowy figure on the other side of the Cadillac. The bullets either missed or went right through him. Two silver blurs zipped across the rearview mirror. The goon went stiff, squeezed off a shot aimlessly into the sky. Two throwing knives protruded from his eye sockets. The goon cried tears of blood as he fell over dead.

Gator drew his snub-nosed revolver. The other goon pulled his own Glock and rushed out to check on his fallen comrade.

"Damn it, get back here," Gator shouted.

In a blind rage the goon charged Glock first, firing wildly toward the Cadillac, though the assassin was no longer in sight. "Where'd he go?" The goon spun frantically in place, searching for the assassin while he ejected the empty clip and slammed in a new one.

Ramon heard a thud on the roof of the Cuda.

"He's above us, Dad."

The assassin sprang from the roof, and with a gliding leap descended upon the goon. A long blade extended from the assassin's sleeve, and with it he cleaved the goon's head clean off. It wobble-rolled into the garage, leaving a bloody streak across the floor.

The assassin faded into the shadows.

Gator abandoned his sanctuary behind Isaac and backstepped toward the side door. The revolver trembled in his hand as he swept it back and forth, unsure where to point it. As he opened the door, he came face to face with the assassin. He backed up, aimed the revolver at the assassin, but before he could get off a shot, the wraith easily slapped the gun from his hand. "Where do you think you're going?"

Ramon felt a chill. That gravelly voice could have easily come from the depths of hell itself.

"What do you want?" Gator shouted. "I've given up everything for the Syndicate, my friends, my dignity, for money and glory that was never mine to have."

The assassin grabbed Gator by the collar and shoved him across the garage to the opposite wall, pinning him. "The Syndicate wants their money."

As he watched the horror show unfold, Ramon muttered, "This is my chance. I'm going to get Isaac."

"No, son. Don't."

Ramon was already out of the car and sprinting for Isaac who was still doubled over in the chair. He reached Isaac in a moment's time and went to loosening the ropes. "Hey, man. It's me, Ramon. I got you."

"Ramon... Awesome race," Isaac muttered and looked at him with swelling eyes and a bloody smile.

"Thanks, man. We can talk about it later. Can you stand up?" Ramon helped Isaac to his feet. He glanced over his shoulder to see if he'd been spotted. "Let's go."

Gator was now pleading for his life. "I'll get the money back. I'll even double it. Tell the Syndicate I need more time."

"It's too late for that. The Syndicate is done giving you more time, Gator. They have plans for your land. Your race track is an eyesore. So killing you works out better for them." The assassin unsheathed a Crocodile Dundee knife and pressed the point to Gator's gut like he was about to bleed a pig.

Ramon and Isaac had almost made it to the car when: "Wait," Gator blurted out. "It's them. They stole the money...stashed it someplace."

The assassin glanced over his shoulder, spotted Ramon and recognized the Dark Coast Racer's car. "You!"

"Go get them," Gator shouted.

The Assassin hissed in Gator's face. "I believe you'd sell your own mother's soul." With a quick thrust and twist, he plunged the blade into Gator's stomach and swiped crossways, loosing his intestines. "The devil's gonna love meeting you."

Gator croaked, gagged, hugged his stomach as if that alone could keep his guts from spilling out further...then he slid down the wall and slumped over in a dying heap.

"Shit." Ramon had one arm under Isaac's shoulder, limping him along when he felt a sharp piercing pain in his back. Two steps to the passenger door, the pain intensified by a factor of one hundred. His knees buckled.

Isaac held him up. "Let go of me. Save yourself."

And then another stabbing pain wracked his body. "Get out of here." He shoved Isaac out of the garage. "Go. Go!"

Two more throwing knives penetrated his

back. Ramon spun around to confront the Assassin, already swiping a bloody knife he'd pulled from Gator's stomach. Ramon lurched backward to avoid the blade, which slashed the leather jacket.

Ramon lunged forward with a headbutt. The Dark Coast Racer helmet smashed into the Assassin's face. He squinched his eyes. His nose looked broken and leaked blood. Ramon thought he just might make it to the car. That thought was short-lived as a bolt of lightning-hot heat struck his shoulder.

The assassin had plunged the blade in deep, so deep the handle broke off.

It had happened so fast, Ramon hadn't time to register the pain and scream. Instinctively he lunged forward again with another headbutt. This time the Assassin caught Ramon's head in the palm of his hand. With a tug and a twist, the Assassin ripped the helmet off and tossed it to the side.

Now he saw Ramon's face. "You're just a kid. You're not the Dark Coast Racer." He actually sounded disappointed.

"That was my dad, you bastard." Ramon mustered enough strength to throw a punch that missed.

The Assassin countered with the wrist sword that slid from his sleeve and stabbed Ramon in the stomach.

He couldn't believe this was happening, to fall victim to the same maniac who'd killed his dad.

The assassin stepped in close and tight.

Ramon felt the tip of the blade exit through his back.

"Your father died better."

"Go to hell." He gasped.

The Assassin leaned in to Ramon's ear. "I'll see you there."

From out of nowhere Isaac rushed in, wielding the Dark Coast Racer helmet like a bowling ball.

"Isaac. No."

He swung with all his might, throwing his whole body into the motion. The blow connected with the Assassin's head, and he stumbled to a workbench where he fell to the floor in a sprawl.

Ramon slumped to the floor. He wanted to feel a sense of relief, but he knew this wasn't the end of it. *A man knows when he's about to die.* Shame he was just a kid with big-man dreams of racing cars, winning trophies, impressing the ladies, and all for not.

"Damn, you look like a pin cushion," Isaac said as pulled the knives out of Ramon's back.

Ramon grimaced. He held his bleeding gut wound and felt woozy.

"Come on." Isaac ushered Ramon toward the loping Cuda.

His legs wobbled and his body screamed in pain from all the stab wounds. He didn't look back to see where the Assassin had gone, but he imagined him right behind them with a sword about to cut him in half.

Ramon made it to driver's side and got in.

Isaac ran to the passenger's side and jumped in. He looked at Ramon with a worried expression. "You good to drive?"

"I'm in better shape than your face." Being back in the Cuda didn't restore his strength as he had hoped. But he still felt like he had enough gas in him to drive them out of there. He just needed to hear his dad's voice. "Dad?"

No dad. Only white-noise buzzed eerily from the speakers, like he was trying to communicate, but the connection was fading.

"Dad? You there?" He coughed a bit as he said it. More blood in his mouth didn't worry him as much as not hearing his dad. Maybe he ran out of time. If so, the Syndicate had won.

"Ramon, look." Isaac pointed to the Assassin advancing toward them. His angry face was a river of blood. The black mist swirled around him.

However, Ramon saw something the Assassin couldn't see. Under that mist, Gator came crawling on his belly, a blade with the gator-skull handle in his hand. *The old hidden blade in the cane trick, so typical of Gator.* Ramon couldn't fathom what Gator had in mind, but being a hero in his last dying moments must've been his plan.

Ramon didn't stick around to see how that final act would end. He threw the car in reverse, rammed Gator's Cadillac, and ploughed it across the parking lot. The Cuda spun around, he shifted to drive, and hit the gas.

"You should drive to a hospital," Isaac shouted.

The Cuda blasted out of the parking lot and on to the main road.

"No. Our shop. There's no way we can explain what happened to us."

#

*"Kill him. Rip him. Make him pay," t*he dark voice commanded Johnny as he pushed himself back to his feet and rubbed his head, aching from the blow.

The friend, Isaac, had nailed him with the helmet while he was having too much fun killing the Racer's son.

How disappointing...he wasn't the original Racer. Still, the thought of having killed a father and a son pleased him.

Johnny smirked, remembering the chain of events that caused him so much joy. He'd pulled out a throwing knife, and seeing the racer and his friend, Isaac, hobbling toward the black car, quickened his pace. He zeroed in on Isaac. The knife would strike point-first through the base of his skull, killing him instantly from a severed spinal cord. Johnny had made the throw countless times. Some kills were just for sport. Some for money. This one was for payback...but he missed. The knife sailed high. Something had snagged his foot and threw off his aim.

The Racer sped off into the night.

Johnny looked down at the nuisance holding his ankle. "Gator! You're not dead yet?" The old fart had belly-crawled, leaving a smear of blood and guts on the concrete floor.

Gator snarled incoherently as he swiped a blade at Johnny's leg.

"I think not." Johnny tugged his leg free of Gator's grasp and pivoted, kicked him in the head, and knocked out a gold tooth. Now he was either unconscious or the rest of the way dead.

Either way, the job's almost done. He picked up a can of gasoline he'd set in the corner.

Johnny doused Gator's body first with the gasoline and then proceeded to pour it on everything from the workbench to the walls. He left a trail of gasoline behind him on his way out, then tossed the empty can aside.

Just like before. It never gets old.

Johnny reached into his coat pocket and pulled out a pack of Lucky Strike cigarettes and stick matches. After he lit a cigarette, and after a long puff, he tossed the match on the trail of gasoline, igniting it with a whoosh.

He watched long enough to see the fire take hold of the garage, took a few more drags off the cigarette then tossed it into the flames. After backing away, he turned and walked to the far end of the parking lot while flipping the coin in the air and catching it. "Heads you live, Isaac. Tails you die."

The coin landed in his palm, heads up. "His lucky night."

#

Isaac had dozed off, probably from the concussion. His face was busted up pretty bad. He had fought off sleep as much as he could, but the brain had shut off. It turned back on when Ramon drove into the industrial compound. He'd parked right next to their future mechanic shop. Isaac moaned, and turning, he discovered he had a crook in his neck. His face hurt so bad, he didn't dare touch it.

He looked to Ramon and noticed he was slumped over, his chin touching his chest and his forehead on the wheel. "Ramon, you did it. You got us here..."

Silence from Ramon.

"Ramon?" Isaac cried. "If you're faking dead, I swear I'm gonna date your mom."

That should've got to him, but silence bathed the car in a sense of dread Isaac had never experienced. He reached over and shook his friend fiercely.

"Ramon. No." He screamed as tears welled in his eyes. He rushed out of the car, and as he headed to the driver side to pull Ramon out, the Cuda ignited into flames. "What in God's name?"

He stumbled away as the red and yellow flames turned glowing blue, and then whirled like a tornado that stretched up into the sky. It sucked up the smoke, the leaves and litter, and in a matter of moments, the burning car with Ramon's body were whisked away, leaving strange blue ashes in its wake that disintegrated in the air before touching the ground.

Isaac looked to the heavens and cried for his friend. And for a moment, he forgot about the hamburger those goons had made of his face.

Chapter 11

Johnny had done his share of the killing tonight. *Time to get home to my family.*

In the last parking space, a blanket of shadows hung a veil of darkness and hid his car from view. He clinched the coin in his hand and waved his other hand over the blanket of shadows. The veil washed away, revealing an Isotta Fraschini Tipo 8A, a luxurious car painted a pearl white without a blemish on her, as though she had just rolled out of the factory in 1928.

Johnny slid the coin into his pocket and himself behind the wheel.

He smirked as he started her up. *Still purrs like a kitten.* He drove out of the parking lot and toward the shadowy forest line along the side of the road. Just before the T8 would have smashed into the trees, the shadows expanded from the forest into a gapping cosmic maw and swallowed the car and Johnny whole.

When he emerged from the shadows, Johnny was driving on another strip of the Dark Coast, three-hundred miles away from the flames and carnage at Gator's Tail Raceway. This road was old, poorly paved and windswept. In either direction, pine trees and Florida overgrowth had taken hold of the landscape. A crumbling brick wall ran along the road and branched off to the beginning of another street never finished. It quickly turned into a dirt trail that led to a dead end, thick with overgrowth in swampy ground. The wall still held up a weathered sign that read: *Welcome to Remote Pines. Thoroughly exclusive living for the modern family.*

Johnny drove straight for the thick overgrowth. Instead of crashing into the brush, the visage of the dead end disappeared, turned two-dimensional, folded away and then returned to form the forest behind him. Johnny had driven through the center point in space and time. He felt nothing but saw a flash of light, and then he was driving through the entrance to Remote Pines. Instead of night, it was day, and instead of the 90s, he was back in his time, 1933, where he had carved out a life for himself and Rose.

Often Johnny thought sarcastically about all the people he had to carve up in the process. The doubloon of darkness that spoke to him, prolonged his life, also granted him the power to preserve this block of what would have been an exclusive urban neighborhood but was left undeveloped. *He didn't have to rub elbows with no one.* Johnny often imagined it as a time capsule where the perfect day never ended. His house was the largest on the block, and three other homes were built in lots adjacent his. Remote Pines had some land that was undeveloped marsh surrounding a pond with a pleasant wooden dock.

One of his neighbors, Robert the doctor, was out past his driveway on the sidewalk, checking his mail. The box was empty, but Robert thumbed through it as though he'd just been visited by the postman. Robert stopped and waved at Johnny as he drove by. He had, in the past, stopped a few times to see where the conversation would go, but it was either about a recent patient or how the newlyweds with the inheritance next door were too loud.

They were loud but not as loud as the scream Robert released when Johnny gutted him. Now Robert was a figment of himself, a ghost, a corporal memory trapped in Johnny's perfect day.

Johnny parked in his driveway. His other neighbor Edward, the bank owner, stood near the hedges that separated his yard and Johnny's. Edward held a garden hose, wagged it side to side as if he were caring for a patch of grass. But no water came out of the hose.

Edward hollered, "Hello, John. Mighty fine

day today."

"Sure, is." Johnny nodded.

"Not as fine as that automobile of yours." He said the same thing every time, and always added a snort-laugh.

Johnny smirked, remembering when he stabbed Edward to death, and how he had snorted then while gurgling on his own blood.

"Thanks." Johnny ducked into the front door before Edward asked him to take the car for a spin.

Dahlia, Johnny's five-year-old daughter, jumped up from the radio, rushed to him, and hugged his leg. "Daddy."

He picked her up and hugged her, then carried her back to the sofa near the radio that was on but emitted no sound. He set her down gently and followed up with a peck on her forehead. From the living room he could hear his wife, Rose, moving in the kitchen.

"Hey, honey." Johnny stood at the entrance where the two rooms met.

Rose turned from her spot by the stove, handling a pan. "Hey, you. Dinner is almost ready. How was work?"

"Killer, as usual." He moved up behind her and hugged her. She leaned in. Johnny glanced into the pan. It was bare. Rose and Dahlia were ghosts too.

"*Was it worth it?*" the darkness asked. "*Killing the ones you loved the most?*"

"I did as you said I had to do in order to save them. It was the only way to keep them perfect forever."

"*Would you do it over?*"

"Without question."

"*Good. That's why I like you, Johnny.*"

Chapter 12

15 years later
Dark Coast circa 2000s

Row exited the hospital. Storm clouds in the distance. Summer thunder. She pulled her cell phone from her pocket. For weeks she had been ignoring notifications. Only glancing at the messages, a couple words at a time, afraid of connecting and being seen when she was at her emotional lowest. Very few people knew her mother was dying from cancer. Now that her mother was dead, Row felt both a deep sadness from the loss but also a sense of relief that her mother's suffering had ended. There was a message from her girlfriends at the car club. They were very superficial texts, the standard.

"Hey, girl. Come hang!"

"Where you been? Everyone misses you!"

"Don't miss this party!"

"We're at the spot. Gavin is here. He wants to see you. He's sooo cute!"

Gavin had been Row's recent boyfriend; he

was the leader of the car club she had been hanging with. They had kissed and she had to stop him from going any further. He had clearly not been told *no* often. He wasn't the kind of guy she could talk with about her mom. Also, Gavin was the kind of guy who wouldn't ask either.

"Hey, babe. Where are you? I have a race tonight. You should come cheer me on."

She exited the text box on her phone and thumbed to the next message. The race could be a good escape. She had been cooped up in the hospital for weeks. The smell and sounds had gotten to her. All the sickness and death. Additionally, Row would never eat hospital mystery meat again.

The sky lit up with a bolt of lightning, jarring her from her thoughts. She appreciated the hot sticky smell of rain on its way. It made her kick herself in gear and start walking toward the bus stop. She didn't dare drive her mom's old Buick. The smell of cigarettes was so heavy on the inside it would trigger Row. Her mom hadn't wanted to hear anything about how secondhand smoke caused cancer. Even after she had gotten her diagnoses. Row had Uncle Isaac take the old Buick to sell or salvage. The thought of her brother's best friend, who'd helped her through his death and life's challenges and earned him the *uncle* endearment, made her remember a text message she had received but not yet opened. Isaac was one of the people who knew about her mom.

She stepped over a pothole in the sidewalk. The street was empty aside from one motorist waiting at a red light and a delivery van parked in an unloading bay across the street under a skyrise.

"Hey, I'm sorry about your mom. I loved her like my own. If you want to talk, come see me at the shop. I have a surprise for you."

She didn't want to talk about her mom, not really. Nothing to say. The surprise, though, interested her.

She stopped under a streetlamp that had just flickered on, as the sun was setting behind the summer thunder clouds.

"Thanks, Uncle Isaac. I'll be there soon." She typed out the text and hit send.

She thumbed to the last few unanswered texts. They were from Jeremy, her childhood friend, maybe her first real crush.

"Hey, I'm sorry about your mom. Let me know if you need anything. I'm here for you."

I'll respond at some point. She exited the text box so she wouldn't have to deal with his fawning over her right now. She had her reasons why she didn't want to talk to or see Jeremy. He brought up nostalgic feelings from her childhood, and those memories only made her sad. She was already bummed enough: about her mom passing, her dad's mysterious death, and even her brother's disappearance. Presumed dead. Maybe the races would lighten her mood.

She pulled up Gavin's text box again and typed: *"Hey, I'll see you at the race tonight."*

She slid the phone in her pant pocket and looked up at the bus stop down the street. Headlights beamed on, and the sound of a V8 engine shattered the calm. It was a black muscle car. The way it slow-rolled toward her caused her nerves to flare.

The car stopped at the curb, right where she was standing on the sidewalk. Row waved it off. "Beat it, buster." She had delt with creeps of the Dark Coast. The tinted passenger window rolled down, revealing the car was empty.

"What the..." She muttered, backing away.

"Row, get in. It's me, Ramon." The voice came from the radio; Row was certain of it. She backed up even farther, stumbled into a trashcan.

The city bus pulled in.

She made a run for it, jumped in through the folding door. As she retrieved her bus pass from her pocket, she looked back at the street. The muscle car rolled away.

The bus driver must have noticed her frantic

behavior. "You okay, miss?"

She nodded yes to him then found a seat in the empty bus.

The bus driver shrugged and carried on.

Was she hallucinating? She knew stress and grief could do a number on the mind, but she hadn't realized it could cause deliria. Her phone vibrated with a new text. It was Gavin. She clicked on it to get her mind off the mysterious car.

"Sweet, see you tonight!"

She grinned and then thought about getting to Isaac's shop. *I wonder what surprise he has for me.*

#

Isaac wiped his hands on the oil rag before looking at the text from Row. He smiled warmly. She had sent the message an hour ago. So she would be walking in at any time. Row was like a sister to Isaac. He had been checking in on her throughout the last fifteen years, ever since Ramon went up in flames. That night had never been forgotten. Plus, the Syndicate money that he had stashed was enough to start his business, I&R Customs, twice over. And the name of the shop was a memorandum for his friend and the dreams they'd shared.

Isaac & Ramon Customs.

Since he opened shop, business around the industrial district had started coming back. A house painting company opened in one of the warehouses. Throughout the weekdays, Vinny, a hotdog vendor, would set up his cart, shaped like a chili dog, on the corner. Warehouse workers and truckers would often stop there for lunch. Isaac was Vinny's best customer. He had helped Vinny with some car repairs for free, and now Isaac ate for free. He wondered how long it would take to get tired of hotdogs for lunch and dinner. A few months later, he was still craving them.

"Hey, Uncle Isaac." He heard Row call from the garage entrance.

Isaac always left the door open whenever he was here. He exited his back office to see Row standing by her surprise that was tarped over. He wondered if she had guessed what she was getting.

"Hey, Row. How are you?" Isaac hugged her. She was stiff at first, but then her demeanor softened, and she hugged him back. He could feel she needed contact the way she held on a little longer after her initial hesitation. She wasn't crying or hadn't been recently, which surprised him. But he had remembered their last serious talk when her mom was on her last few breaths. That Row was all out of tears. She was burnt out emotionally. Though now, Isaac noticed a different look to her: worried, fretful, a glance over her shoulder, a twitch in her brow, like maybe the boogieman might jump out at her. "You want to talk?"

"Yeah, it's been hard on me. I had to sign out moms' body today, for the hospital to release her to the funeral home for cremation. Been catching up on some texts, too....And for some reason I thought about Ramon on the way here."

Isaac wondered if this was the right time to tell her about what really happened to him, and how he never died in an accidental fire at Gator's.

"So you got a surprise for me?"

"Figured that would get you here." Isaac chuckled.

"You know that's not true." She nudged him playfully. "But for real. What is it?"

"You're standing next to it."

Row looked at the tarped vehicle next to her. "You got me a car? No way."

"Nah, just a pile of clothes I want you to take to the dry cleaners." It was a chore he'd given her to do before.

She carefully pulled the tarp off the car to reveal a red 1990 Honda Civic hatchback. "Where did you get this?"

"Some junker I fixed up. The engine was blown. It only took me couple of months. Gave her a new paint job and tinted windows, too."

"It must've cost you a fortune."

"Nah. I sold your mom's old Buick to help

with the funds. Keys are in the ignition, waiting for you."

Row opened the driver door and slid behind the wheel. "How do I look in it?" She started the engine and gave it some gas. The aftermarket turbo whined as the car lurched on its springs. Her smile seemed genuine for the first time in a while.

"Like you two were meant for each other."

Row jumped out and wrapped her arms around Isaac's neck, gave him a big hug. "Thanks, Uncle Isaac."

"You're welcome, Row. You gonna take her for a spin?"

"There's a car club meeting tonight, perfect time to show off my new ride at a street race."

Isaac remembered her brother, Ramon, and his obsession with racing. He fought off tears, hoping Row wouldn't be so reckless. "You be careful. She's fast."

"I'm hungry."

"Vinny hasn't closed the hotdog cart, yet."

"You buying?" She pulled out the keys from the ignition.

"Yeah, it's on me, kid." She didn't know he ate free.

Chapter 13

That night, Row drove her Honda to the car club. They met after hours at a strip mall in the red-light district. At least twenty cars were gathered, a handful of motorcycles, and some low-rider trucks were parked on display, too. One of the low-riders was blasting the trunk stereo system. Three cars were lined up for a race. Gavin's Lancer was one.

Row pulled her Honda to the racing line without making herself known. The tinted windows kept her secret. Her anonymous arrival turned heads and made the crowd point as if in wonder at who she was. Butterflies flitted in her stomach. She had second thoughts, never raced before, though she'd seen others do it. *No, I'm done as a spectator.*

A flashy dressed guy wearing sunglasses and a yellow hoodie stepped forward with a bullhorn. "Alright, alright. We got a four-way race. Rain's coming. First one around the strip mall and back wins the pot of gold at the end of the rainbow." He held up a wad of cash.

Gavin was staring her way as if to see who was

behind the wheel. His curiosity made Row smirk. She wondered how Gavin would take losing to her. She imagined him impressed and lifting her up in his arms to congratulate her. Another image followed, of him butthurt and not talking to her for a few days. He'd have to get over it.

"Racers, are you ready?" He raised three fingers. "Three, two, one." He dropped his arm with a dramatic flourish.

Row gave it the gun, shifted, clutch and gas. The turbo screamed. Slammed her back in her seat. She could hardly breathe. Shifted.

She and Gavin were neck-and-neck as they took the first turn around the strip mall. Gavin careened his Lancer toward the side of her Honda. Fearing he'd sideswipe her and scratch the new paint job, she hit the brakes, downshifted, and let him take the lead as she switched gears and hugged his bumper. On the straightaway, she floored the gas. The turbo screamed and she flew past the Lancer. In the next turn, she held the lead by drifting around the corner at full throttle.

After blowing across the finish line, she hit the brakes. The Honda skidded a full circle. She hit the gas and gave it one more victory spin. By that time, Gavin's Lancer careened to a stop in front of her, and the other two cars drove out of the parking lot. She laughed at Gavin jumping out of his car. He angrily kicked gravel and threw down his racing gloves as he stormed toward her. *Won't he be surprised to see me?*

Some of the car club members ran from the crowd to surround him, which slowed his advance. Row noticed one of them was Lucy, a girlfriend who had texted her during her absence from the club. She seemed especially attentive to Gavin, very close, an arm around his waist, lips to his ear.

The crowd gathered around her Honda, pumping their fists in the air and cheering. Row stayed in the car to enjoy the attention everyone was showing her. Many of them prodded her join in the celebration. "Come on out." "Who are you?" "Great race." "We want to see your engine."

Gavin seemed to have cooled off, most likely something Lucy had told him, and now seemed eager to meet the anonymous racer who had won. He was smiling toward the Honda and nodding.

Row finally gave in and got out of the car.

Gavin's jaw dropped.

Lucy quickly took her arm from around his waist and looked away. The guy with the bullhorn met her at the open door. "Congratulations, Row. Good race." He handed her a wad of cash. "Three-hundred dollars."

Row walked through a gauntlet of pats on her shoulders and hand clapping to get to Gavin.

"Surprise."

"What the hell, Row?" He looked angry again, but more alarming, his eyes were bloodshot like he was drunk or high or both. "You ghost me and the club for weeks. Then you text me you're coming to the race. I thought you were coming to watch me...not humiliate me."

"Are you serious, Gavin?" Okay. His pride was hurt, obviously, but his anger was very unattractive. She offered him a handshake. "We good?"

He batted her hand away. "Bitch, don't touch me."

"What did you call me?"

"Bitch! You're a bitch." He slapped her with the back of his hand in the mouth.

She spat blood and swung a fist across his face. "Don't you ever—"

"What in the fuck, Row?" He held his jaw.

Lucy embraced him like he was a hurt puppy.

"You're nothing but a cheating bastard. Lucy, how could you?"

"That's it." Gavin rushed to his trunk, pulled out a crowbar and baseball bat. He tossed the bat to a nearby club member. Gavin led him to her Honda and broke the windshield, the side mirrors, and back window. With the pointed tip of the crowbar, Gavin started puncturing the tires. Two other club members joined in, jumping and stomping on the hood and roof, denting it all to hell.

Row rushed to Gavin and yanked him around. "That's enough," she cried out but showed no tears.

He knocked her back with his elbow.

She balled a fist.

Lucy and two of her friends grabbed her by the arms and dragged her away from Gavin. She smelled alcohol on their breaths, which explained their behavior toward her, too. "Let go of me."

A flash of lightning. A crack of thunder. The rain started pouring down.

The crowd started to disburse as if it was Armageddon. Every person for themselves. Crews gathered and split. A few people were trampled on the way to their rides.

The chaos and rain didn't stop Gavin. A few more kicks to her door; a few more crowbar strikes to her windows. Glass shattered. Metal creaked. The guy with the baseball bat went insane on the headlights and grill. Within moments, her car was completely trashed, and her heart was completely broken.

Gavin and his crew scattered. Lucy and her friends let Row go and fled after Gavin.

Row felt as battered as her car looked. Her lip was swelling, bleeding, but she refused to cry. The Honda would still run, but it would need four new tires, new glass and a ton of body work.

Gavin sped by in his Lancer. "You're membership is revoked." He was laughing as he rolled up the window.

The car show was over. Everyone had left. The thudding sound of the bass in a car stereo faded in the distance, leaving just the patter of the rain on the pavement. She sank to her knees in a puddle. The weight of her mother's death, combined with the betrayal of all her friends, hit her harder than anything she'd ever endured.

I'm truly alone. Finally, her tears let loose, to mix with the raindrops sliding down her face, the misery flooding her heart, a tsunami, total devastation.

Headlights beamed on. The distinct rumble of the V8 engine from the black-muscle car cut through the rain. It was the same driverless hotrod from earlier. Row wiped her eyes, wondering if she was really seeing it again. The car rolled up to her and stopped. The driver's door opened, and the cab light came on. Still no driver.

The radio buzzed, then: *"Come on, Row. Get in."* It sounded like her brother's voice. She had been a kid when he passed away from a mysterious fire at Gator's Tail Raceway. Though she had fond memories of Ramon, they weren't strong enough for her to jump into a freaky driverless car.

"You're not alone, kid."

How did he know? Row thought of salvation at hand, considered that the forces at play in the Dark Coast might be stronger than anyone realized, and that she needed to have faith in her brother. Maybe more than anything she was curious about what the hell was going on. Was she finally going crazy?

"You're not going crazy, Row. Get in."

After getting to her feet, she faced the idling hotrod. "What do you want from me?"

"I need you. Get in. I'll tell you all about it."

At the very least, she needed a ride home. Slowly got her drenched self into the driver seat. As she took hold of the wheel, a shock of lightning went through her, it seemed. Her wet clothes dried and black riding leathers formed over them. A racing helmet appeared on her head with its visor down. She glanced in the rearview mirror. "I look like a ninja NASCAR driver. Am I hallucinating?"

"No."

She steadied her hands, now clad in racing gloves.

"How does it feel, sis?"

"Ramon...is it really you?"

"Yes. How about a little payback against those car club fools?"

She thought about Gavin and his crew, laughing on their getaway. The feeling of betrayal.

Her Honda sitting in a wrecked heap. Payback felt like the right thing to do. Would it cure everything? Would it bring her mom back? She knew better, but she would savor the feeling or justified retribution, nonetheless.

"Okay. Payback. That's what I want."

"Drive."

#

Gavin was bummed. Row was hotter than Lucy or any of the other girls in the car club. And he thought they were finally hitting it off a month ago. Now she had to learn a lesson. No one ghosted him and then showed up to beat him in front of the whole club. *Plus, she hit me. How humiliating.*

"She had it coming, Gavin," Lucy said to him, hanging on his arm.

The bitch. He had gathered everyone together in a parking lot on the other side of the red-light district. The rain had stopped. They had parked their cars with the headlights on as lighting for their hangout, furnished with old sofas they'd scrounged from homeless encampments. Some of the crew were building a wooden table but ran out of nails. The Krager brothers had brought beer in an ice cooler, of which they'd already knocked down half before the race.

Gavin crushed an empty can he had polished off and threw it into the parking lot. "Toss me another one," he said to one of his club members who was digging around in the cooler.

"You still have to drive me home," Lucy said.

He cracked open the beer and gulped it. "I'll be fine. The cops have to catch—"

The sound of a revving engine erupted in the distance, cutting him off. He heard screeching tires and saw headlights speeding toward his Lancer.

"What the hell?"

A black muscle car barreled out of the darkness and slammed into the Lancer, sending a tornado of metal and glass whirling through the air as the Lancer rolled and flipped like it was a stunt in an action movie.

"My car," Gavin yelled, throwing the beer can at the hotrod as it busted a U-turn and stopped, now facing the hangout. The powerful engine loped. The car rocked on its springs. He grabbed a hammer off the ground and held it up. "Come on. What are you waiting for?"

The other club members stood stunned in place, even as the muscle car lurched forward in an explosion of thunder and screamed toward them. This time it slammed into one of the low-rider trucks and sent it spinning into the other club cars before it tumbled across the parking lot. Some of the members took off running.

Gavin, Lucy, and the other holdouts huddled

within the circle of sofas, watching in wide-eyed horror as the muscle car careened a one-eighty and made a beeline straight for them.

Gavin threw the hammer. It bounced off the windshield. In a split second he realized the futility of his defense, as the car hadn't been the least bit damaged by all the demolition it had dished out. "Who the hell are you?"

Lucy screamed. "Oh my god. He's going to kill us."

"Get out of my way." Gavin shoved past Lucy and the others and ran for his life.

The muscle car smashed through the sofas. Splinters, cushion fluff, ice, and beer cans flew everywhere. Gavin dived into a puddle to duck the flying debris. Lucy left him there to watch the hotrod's taillights fade into the darkness. Even in his drunken state, he knew his car club was wrecked beyond belief. The parking lot looked like a junk yard. Worse, he didn't know who had taken him down. Or why? He'd never seen that black Barracuda before. Hoped he'd never see it again. The devil had come calling, of that he was sure.

Flashing and sirens.

"Damn. Dark Coast Five-O." Gavin lowered his head and cried, too defeated to get up and run.

Chapter 14

Row couldn't believe it. The thrill and adrenaline rush that came from driving such an indestructible car made her feel more alive than ever. The grief over her mother's death had been pushed to the farthest edges of her mind.

"So, this car is supernatural?" she asked the radio while driving away from the devastation she had caused on the car club. In the rearview mirror, she saw police lights converging on the parking lot, though shrinking as she sped farther down the street.

"That's the Dark Coast for you."

She stopped at a red light, let silence fill the car. She didn't feel alone at the moment, but the feeling felt odd. Like it wasn't real or tainted with her own emotions. She heard the voice of her brother coming through the speakers and felt like she should have had more questions for him. Or more to say, like telling him about mom's last days. *Is he calling to me from the afterlife?*

"That's one way to describe it. A call from the afterlife."

"You can hear my thoughts?"

"It's hard to explain. When you're in range of the car, you feel my psychic pull. And now that you're the Dark Coast Racer, we share a quantum connection. I'm sorry about mom. I wish I could have been there with you."

"Is mom with you...there, in the afterlife?"

"It doesn't work that way. But while I'm here with you, I'm grounded on earth. I'm kind of in a room by myself."

"Why did you come back... in a car, no less." The red light turned green, and she accelerated through the intersection, smooth and slow as a little old lady.

"This is our dad's car. And it's not a choice. This shit just happened. The Dark Coast is full of weird, unexplainable phenomena. This one has to do with the Syndicate."

"The Dark Coast Mafia? What did they do?"

"It's getting late. We should get this car off the streets for now. Head to Isaac's shop. He hasn't closed up yet."

"Great. He's going to love to hear about the Honda getting trashed."

"I'm sure that will be an afterthought once he hears my voice."

"Good point."

#

Isaac heard the unmistakable sound of an approaching Hemi V-8, a kind of thunder trapped between his ears. A memory of horror and death fought to push that sound back into the darkest corner of his mind. He turned his attention away from the engine he was building to look out the open garage door. A black 1970 Plymouth Barracuda crept into the shop, a vision he thought he'd never see again. "No way." His mouth hung open. "It's impossible." Fifteen years ago, he had watched that car swirl up into the sky, in flames, and take Ramon with it. The torque wrench trembled in his hand then clanked on the floor.

The car stopped just inside the garage door. The walls rattled until the engine shut off, and then the headlights went dark. He couldn't see who was behind the wheel. Before he could ask, the driver door swung open and a leather-clad driver stepped out. Helmet, gloves, the whole getup Ramon had worn, but it wasn't a fit young man in that small, curvy outfit. The hair on his neck prickled.

She took off the helmet and flung her hair loose.

"Row!" *Something is terribly wrong here.* "What is going on?"

"I'm not sure you'd believe me."

"Your father's ghost car showed up fifteen years ago with your brother, and now it's returned

~100~

with you to carry out the family legacy. What's not to believe?"

"Well, that about sums it up. Ramon told me to come here."

"Ramon talked to you?"

"Yeah. Through the radio."

Isaac walked to the car, slowly circled it and ran his fingertips over the quarter panels, back deck, fender, and the hood. It felt the same fifteen years ago: cold, smooth, and tingly, as if supernaturally charged by some otherworldly force. He thought about opening the hood to see the Hemi underneath.

The Dark Coast Racer's warning came back in a rush. *"No. Never open the hood."* Ramon's dad had spoken through the radio. Now Isaac wondered if Ramon would speak to him the same way.

He opened the passenger door and sat inside. Though he'd left the door open, the black interior trim, black vinyl buckets, the black center console, black shifter, blacked-out dash, the dark tinted windows themselves rushed at him, plunging his mind back to the night he'd been beaten all to hell by Gator's goons and Ramon was stabbed to death by the Assassin. The trigger was bad enough that he had to fight the urge to leap out and dodge the flood of emotions. He had to know... "Ramon. Are you here?"

"Hey, Isaac." Ramon's voice buzzed through the speakers. "I hear you loud and clear."

Goosebumps blossomed on Isaac's arms. "What are you doing?"

Row stooped to the open door. "I told you so."

"Awesome job on the shop, Isaac. You pulled it off."

"That stash of Syndicate money didn't hurt."

"Wait," Row piped up. "What money?"

"How about those Jaguars?" Isaac put in.

"What's been going on with them?"

"They don't have football there, huh?"

"They got nothing here," Ramon said.

Row jumped in. "I want to know what we're doing here."

"The Syndicate has been a boil plaguing the Dark Coast for a century. Dad got tangled up with them, sideline jobs mostly, driving personnel to meetings, and some deliveries, on account of his fast car. He could outrun any police pursuit."

"And a legend was born," Isaac added.

"Gator betrayed him, set him up, and the Syndicate's assassin killed him. Ten years later, our dad came back on a mission to take down the Syndicate. He recruited my help, same as I contacted you, Row. The Assassin killed me too."

Row gasped. "You're saying you want me to help you get Dad's revenge?"

"We've got to take out the Assassin first."

Isaac threw up his arms and huffed. "Great."

"How? Why?"

The radio buzzed. "He's a serial killer...taken hundreds more lives. The Syndicate's top hit-man."

"Come on, Ramon," Isaac shouted. "Your dad failed. You failed. How can we fare better?"

"Somebody has to do it."

"That guy isn't even human."

"He bleeds."

"But he doesn't bleed easy. Besides...he's got all those damn knives."

"Knives?"

"What do you think, Row?" Ramon said. "Wouldn't taking down an Assassin be epic?"

"I wondered what I'd do after high school, didn't know mom's diagnosis would derail my future...but a mission to avenge you and dad sounds better than going the college party route and street racing with a bunch of dumbasses."

"Row. No." Isaac looked pale enough that he might pass out. "That guy is dangerous."

"Does anyone know who this guy is?"

Isaac shrugged, resigned to his fate. He wasn't going to let her go up against the Assassin alone. "There's a podcast called Dark Coast to Coast. Mitch Mills had done an episode a few months ago, talked about the Dark Coast Slasher. The more he talked about the case, the more it reminded me of the Assassin."

"We fought our asses off that night." Ramon's voice came through the radio.

"Don't forget. The guy had superpowers or something. Not human. Possessed for sure."

"Didn't you tell the authorities?" Row asked, trying to follow along.

"No way. With Dark Coast's track record of botchery and corruption? The cops wouldn't have believed us. Not even your mom would have believed that Ramon had become the Dark Coast Racer, let alone that he was killed by a Syndicate assassin with shadow powers. Besides, the Syndicate had the cops in their back pocket. They had to play it off as a tragic fire at Gator's. There was no body found, no death to explain. It all got swept under the rug."

"I get it...don't trust the police. So, we need to listen to this podcaster Mills guy."

"I can help there. I can access his archived episodes." Ramon said, and the radio buzzed with static and then switched to the sound of rock guitar intro music.

"Hello, Dwellers and any newer listeners. Welcome to the Dark Coast to Coast podcast, your place for all the weird and strange happenings in our little corner of the multiverse. I'm here to collect the wildest tales and pass them on to you. Are monsters real? Do aliens visit us from the cosmos? And our continuing story for this episode, who is the Dark Coast Slasher?"

"Yeah. Who?" Row put in.

"As always, we have a doozy for you. This information comes from one of our top sources, Beach Rat Queen. As a former investigative reporter, she has talents for connecting patterns and unearthing clues. She has brought to my attention her research on the Dark Coast Slasher. As if a serial killer in our already creepy and haunted state wouldn't be bad enough, how about if he's immortal? Yeah. Beach Rat Queen has connected his kills going all the way back to the 1930s.

"Now wait, you may be asking, immortal? Remember, in the Dark Coast, nothing is as it seems.

"Our first case dates back to a body count of six in Old Port, the first of the Dark Coast Slasher's massacres. The victims belonged to a small-time outfit called the Rascals connected to the notorious Syndicate. They ran The Blind Tiger Speakeasy at a time when Florida had strict anti-alcohol laws. The crew were all killed in similar fashion, gutted and stabbed.

"Then there came a string of slayings along the Dark Coast that matched that MO. Because most of the victims were criminals, the crimes were never taken as seriously.

"In 1938, in an exclusive community for the wealthy upper class, everyone was found stabbed to death. Sometime later, the abandoned neighborhood of Remote Pines *disappeared.* Many speculated that the marsh had swallowed the suburb, which was still under construction.

"One thing about the Dark Coast is clear. The authorities can't solve these murder cases. According to Beach Rat Queen, the killer had been seen driving a flashy white luxury car from the 1920's era. They haven't even been able to trace the rare car. And throwing knives of the same design, were found at three of the crime scenes, but the cops couldn't determine who manufactured them. Handmade, they decided. Another dead end.

"Beach Rat Queen thinks the Dark Coast Slasher works for the Syndicate. He's possessed by a supernatural force that has tainted the Dark Coast since its beginning. Most likely he's immortal. Now I'll take some calls to see what you Dwellers think about this story, and if you're texting your comments, I'll take a look at those, too."

The radio switched off. "Yeah," Ramon said. "Supernatural sounds just like our assassin."

"Immortal?" Isaac and Row shared terrified expressions.

Row rubbed her arms. "That gives me goosebumps. If he was killing in the 30s that would make him nearly a hundred. So maybe he is immortal." She shrugged. "But I don't like the idea of an evil force plaguing Florida.

"Can't be some old geezer offing people," Isaac said.

"Plus, the assassin that killed me said that he had killed our dad, too. He didn't look like an old man."

Isaac nodded. "And he moved like a ghost."

"Okay. So how do we take him out?" Row asked.

"We draw him into the open and take him down," Ramon responded.

"Easy for you to say from inside a radio." She scoffed. "I want a plan."

"There's the Dark Rock Hotel & Casino," Isaac said. "The Syndicate runs the place. It was built on Gator's Race Way land. If the Dark Coast Racer shows up there, the Syndicate will be left with no choice but to call in their top hitman to handle the problem."

"Okay, so how do we get in?"

"There's a big gambling championship in a few days. They hold it every year. It's open to the public. That would be the perfect time."

Row chimed in. "We should loop in the

podcaster. Maybe he can help broadcast a challenge to the Slasher."

"Good thinking, Row. Let's call him."

"I'll pull up his number." Ramon's voice switched off and suddenly the car speakers emitted a telephone ring. It rang several times and gave a beep noise.

"Hello, you've reached Mitch Mills of Dark Coast to Coast. Leave your name, number, and your story, and I'll get back to you as soon as I can."

"I can send him an instant message, too."

"How are you online from inside the radio?" Isaac asked.

"This car harbors many mysteries. Instant Messenger is showing Mitch Mills inactive, though."

"It's really late. Maybe he called it a night."

"We can continue scheming tomorrow. You and Row can stay here. Oh. Where did you leave the Honda?"

Isaac looked to Row, and noticed she had fallen asleep on the back seat.

That left Ramon to break the bad news about the Honda.

Chapter 15

The next day, Row awoke on a sofa. She could smell coffee brewing. The Cuda sat dark and foreboding in front of the closed garage door. The ceiling lights were off, but high windows shone daylight down on a engine bolted to a roller stand, not three feet away, and a bench strewn with tools. Mechanics had a strange sense of décor.

Isaac stepped up with two steaming mugs. "You still take your coffee with more creamer than coffee, right?"

"You know me, Uncle Isaac." She sat up, crossed her legs, and accepted the coffee with both hands.

"In another hour, Vinny will set up the hotdog cart, and we can grab your favorite chilidogs."

"Yummy."

Isaac sipped his coffee and started circling the Cuda.

"Isaac." Ramon's voice sounded from the radio. "What are you thinking?"

"Nothing."

"I know that face, and it means you're up to

something."

Row noticed it too, now. He had a mischievous expression.

"Well, I couldn't sleep all that well last night because I couldn't stop thinking about something."

"What?"

"What's under the hood, Ramon?"

"It's not a good idea to look, like my dad had warned last time."

"Come on. It can't hurt." Isaac started to finger around under the hood to find the release latch. "I won't touch anything."

"Isaac. I'm warning you."

"Uncle Isaac. You should listen to him," Row said and sipped her coffee.

"Nah, it'll be fine. I'll just take a picture of the Hemi." Isaac released the latch and lifted up the hood.

A swirling vortex of energy reared up to confront him. Macabre faces of ghostly splayed skin and blacked-out eyes screamed with the sudden sound of a powerful Hemi V-8. Total shock and fear glued his shoes to the floor. He couldn't breathe. He couldn't look away. Where was the internal combustion engine with eight pistons, eight spark plugs, sixteen valves, and one tall supercharger? There was no visible place to add oil or antifreeze...just spirit arms reaching out with bony, grasping fingers to grab him and drag him into the vortex where he imagined being fed upon by the lost and tormented souls swimming in this gate to hell.

Suddenly, something jerked him backwards, stumbled, saw the hood slam down, heard the V-8 engine die. He shook his shoulders to free himself from the hands that had a vise-like grip on his arms. Cranking himself around, he caught a glimpse of Row stumbling back and crashing into the sofa. He released the breath he had been holding. "Row. What did I do? I'm sorry."

Row looked at him confused, her eyes wide. "You still want that picture?"

"Told you so," Ramon chimed in.

"Holy mother of God..." Isaac uttered the words but had no idea where they came from: his mind, his heart, maybe even his soul...deep in his soul. He seriously considered heading straight for church. "You saved my ass, Row."

"You should have listened to my brother."

"I did... I didn't... I think... I don't know what happened."

"So, how about that chilidog?" Row finished off her last slurp of coffee.

"You didn't see that, did you?"

"I saw the hood coming down on your head. It about decapitated you. I'm hungry."

He glanced out the narrow window on the garage door. "Vinny is setting up now. After we eat, we can take the tow truck to grab your Honda. Can't let it stay out there in the redlight district for too long."

"Then we'll find Mitch Mills," Row said.

The radio responded, "I'll handle contacting him. I have an idea. I'll let you know if it works when you get back."

#

"There it is." Row pointed to her smashed Honda.

"Geeze, you really pissed off someone."

"They were assholes."

"Your boyfriend?"

"Not anymore."

"Be right back." Isaac got out of the tow truck and went to work latching the hook and cable to the Honda's frame.

The thought of her and Gavin being over made her think of Jeremy and his unanswered texts. Why was she thinking of him now? Were they really an option for a friends to lovers side plot? He had been the only other person she had trusted to talk about her mother's death, aside from Isaac.

Row reached into her pocket for her cellphone and thumbed the home screen. She read it again. *Hey, I'm sorry about your mom. Let me know if you need anything. I'm here for you."*

"Hey," Row typed. "Thanks for your text. Sorry I didn't get back to you right away." She hit send.

Within a minute, her phone vibrated with Jeremey's response. "All good. How are you holding up?"

Her heart tumbled a little. He had a way of making her feel sad.

"Not easy. Been going through stuff. Really been walled off from everyone."

"Don't be hard on yourself. You don't owe anyone. But me, course, for times you made me play Barbies when we were kids."

She stifled a laugh and fought the memories creeping in. Her childhood was gone. Her teens were history. Adulthood was off to a rocky start. And he brings up Barbie dolls. Those were carefree years before Ramon died. Her innocence died with him. Bad boyfriends. Wrecked cars. Assassins... Tears welled. *When am I going to catch a break?* Maybe the Dark Coast supernatural forces were at work. Jeremy's text not coincidental, but divine intervention. She sniffled. Blinked tears. And soldiered on. "lol," She typed. "Don't act like you didn't like playing with Ken riding shotgun in my Barbie mobile."

"I still have nightmares about it."

The tow truck jolted slightly as the hydraulic winch pulled the Honda onto the flatbed. She looked out the back window, saw Isaac tightening the wheel straps to lock the vehicle in place for transport.

Back to texting Jeremy. "Poor boy."

Isaac jumped in the driver's seat and looked at Row. "It's going to cost several thousand dollars to fix it."

"I'm so sorry, Uncle Isaac. Gavin is such a jerk."

"Maybe I'll just take it out of his hide."

"He's not worth it. Just junk the car, cut your losses. I really appreciate the effort and thought you put into it."

"And love." Isaac started driving out of the red-light district.

The phone buzzed. *"You owe me, girl."*

"I owe you what?"

"One real date."

Dread gripped her throat. *What is he doing? Does he know about her breakup with Gavin? Does he think he can just move right in? Is it right? Was she giving him cues? Is it the Dark Coast's idea of a bad joke?* She had to admit, he'd made her forget about herself for the moment. Now she felt guilty that she wasn't feeling sorry for herself. Thinking of what her and Jeremy had been...what they could be when she was a day away from a vigilante suicide mission, seemed a fool's folly. Did she even have a future to share a date with Jeremy? She didn't know if she would survive facing the assassin. Her dad didn't...nor did her brother. *How can I explain it to Jeremy? Should I even try?*

"You okay over there, Row?" Isaac asked. His question broke into her tangled web of thoughts. She just realized she'd been staring out the window.

"Yeah, I think so, Uncle Isaac. Just thinking about the mission."

"I think you're crazy. Runs in your family, though."

She didn't tell him she was scared to death.

As the tow truck turned into the warehouse district, she texted Jeremy. "I'll think about that date. TTYL"

#

Mitch Mills, podcaster extraordinaire, adjusted in his desk chair and sipped his morning coffee. He corrected the positions of his Wolfman and Dracula figurines where they were knocked out of place when he bumped the desk with his knee. On Instant Messenger, he had a chat box invite from:

"The Dark Coast Racer."

Why does that name sound familiar? Then he wondered why everyone had to have the Dark

Coast tagline. It's getting old to the point of cliché. *Maybe I should change the name of my podcast.*

He minimized the chat box and did a web search on the Dark Coast Racer. Scrolling through the first few articles, he quickly realized this guy was some kind of local racing legend loosely linked to the Syndicate. *He's also been missing for twenty-five years and presumed dead...*until, the most recent e-tabloid linked the reincarnated Racer to the fire that burned down Gator's Tail Raceway, which later became the site for Florida's largest casino: the Dark Rock Hotel. He felt a chill. *I need to talk to this guy.* He brought up the chat box.

"*Hello, Mitch Mills?*" the text read.

"Hi." Mitch typed and hit send.

"*I liked your episode on the Slasher.*"

Interesting. That episode was months ago. I better message Beach Rat Queen.

"Are you the Slasher?" was the first thing Mitch thought to ask.

He clicked on his contacts for Instant Messenger. The display of little icons of pixelated people popped up on the screen. Anyone presently online had a green dot below their waving icon. Beach Rat Queen was always green and waving, it seemed, which made reaching out to her easy.

"*I want him stopped same as you.*"

"I see. Both local legends. Both keep showing

up. Are you really the Dark Coast Racer?"

"I am."

"What exactly do you want with the Slasher?"

"Vengeance."

Mitch got goosebumps on his arms. *Now this is getting podcast worthy.*

Mitch screen-printed from his keyboard to copy their exchange and clicked over to the Beach Rat Queen's chat box. There, he pasted the picture of his screen and typed 'urgent' before hitting send.

In seconds, the chat box indicated Beach Rat Queen was typing. Then: *"What's the Dark Coast Racer want with you?"*

"Don't know yet. Do you want to be in the loop?"

"I'm highly fascinated. If it's for real, we could be dealing with a hyper spectral phenomenon that strikes residual, vengeful, and interactive."

"It could be a guy trolling me, too. It's happened. I'll see what the Racer wants and get back to you."

"Bet it's a dozy."

Mitch clicked over to the Dark Coast Racers chat box. "Let's say I believe you, Mr. Racer. What do you want from me?"

"I want your help to draw the Slasher out of his rat hole and trap him.

"Why?"

"Got an old family score to settle."

"If I agree, I want an exclusive on *that* story."

"Why would you hesitate? This mystery is right up your alley."

"I don't want the Syndicate to put a target on my back. Why should I risk my life for you?"

"Not for me...for truth and justice. Isn't that your mantra?"

He got me, damn. "What's your plan?"

"Do another episode on him, but this time claim he failed to kill the Racer."

That gave Mitch a jolt. "Did he really?"

"He killed my dad and me. But we need the Syndicate to think he wasn't successful."

"You got any proof?"

"Are you going to help me or not?"

This story could propel his podcast into the national spotlight. He glanced at Beach Rat Queen's flashing chat box. If anything went south, she'd have his back. "Okay. Let's hear it. The plan."

"Tie the Slasher and the Syndicate to the Dark Coast Racer. That'll piss them off. Then challenge him, in my name, to the gambling championship at their Dark Rock Hotel & Casino."

"This weekend?"

"Yes."

"How do you know he's a gambler?"

"He's not. He's a killer. And he'll want to take us

both out."

Mitch swallowed hard. "That's not very comforting, Racer."

"We'll apprehend him first. Trust me."

He shuddered. *What won't I do for a story?* Mitch took a screen shot and pasted it into Beach Rat Queen's chat box.

She responded right away. *"If there's a connection between the Racer and the Slasher, the plan might work. I say we help him."*

"Okay," Mitch replied. "Okay. But you're in on this one with me. From start to finish. I'm looking forward to meeting you in person."

Beach Rat Queen was typing longer than usual before finally posting: *"Likewise."*

Mitch switched back to the Racer's chat box. "I'll get the word out on social media. Send out a newsletter to the Dwellers that we're going live in a few hours on the Dark Coast Slasher vs Racer episode. How far are you from the Dark Hills area?"

"I'm never far from anywhere."

#

When Row and Isaac got back to I&R Customs, Vinny was at his cart.

"You got any chilidogs left, Vinny?" Isaac called out the window as he was backing the tow truck up to a vacant spot in front of the shop.

"You going to ever get tired of my hotdogs?"

"Never."

"If I started charging you again, I bet you'd be singing a different tune."

Isaac turned red and looked at Row riding shotgun. The glare in her eyes told him she'd heard—

"Free? You made me think you were buying my lunch."

"You want a chilidog or not?"

She laughed. "Of course."

"Then go grab us two while I unload the Honda."

They met up back inside and Row had already finished half her chilidog. She handed Isaac his lunch.

"Thanks for not eating mine, too."

"You'd just get another free one tomorrow."

"Yeah, yeah. I'll have to hear about that for a while."

They sat on the sofa and ate their chilidogs together.

"Hey, you two." Ramon's voice came over the radio. "While you were gone, I made some connections."

"Did Mitch respond?" Isaac asked.

"Yes. I told him I had to make the Slasher think I was still alive. He put out a podcast with me as his guest. We challenged the Slasher, and he called in. I saved the recording." Ramon switched channels.

"Let's take another call. Hello, caller. You're on the air with Mitch Mills and our special guest the Dark Coast Racer."

"Stop talking about me. I'm warning you. Do not repeat anything Beach Rat Queen has said. Or I'll kill you. Hunt you down, cut you and queeny and this want-to-be Dark Coast Racer."

"Slow down there, buddy. Mitch Mills doesn't take threats lightly. You say you're the Dark Coast Slasher. Can you prove it?"

"You'll know for sure when I slash your throat open."

"What do you think, Racer? Is this guy for real?"

"Sounds a bit melodramatic to me. More like a blowhard. Let's take another caller."

"Who's under the Racer's helmet this time? I already killed the first Racer and his son."

"What. Did. You. Say?" Ramon's tone changed from disbelief to anger.

"You're dead. Your father, too. Why don't you Racers stay dead? How many times must I stab you? How many times must I burn you to cinders. You're nothing but an imposter. A cheat."

"It's him," Ramon whispered to Mitch.

"Hey, buddy...ah...Mister Slasher, you aren't the first villain to call my podcast. I once had a vampire god

from Bone Valley—"

"*I'll gut you, Racer, cut you open and rip out—*" The call disconnected.

"*Well, Dwellers,*" Mitch rattled on. "*Join me and Beach Rat Queen for episode three of the Dark Coast Slasher live podcast at the Dark Rock Hotel and Casino. How about you, Racer?*"

"*I'll be there.*"

Ramon switched off the recording. "He aims to kill you, sis. You sure you're up to it?"

Her face turned ghostly white. "He's got to be stopped."

Chapter 16

In Remote Pines, Johnny shot up from the sofa, knocking a glass of whiskey off the end table. He heard his daughter stop playing upstairs. His wife's shuffling in the kitchen ceased.

The podcaster was still on the air. *"Well, Dwellers. Join me and Beach Rat Queen for episode three of the Dark Coast Slasher live podcast at the Dark Rock Hotel and Casino. How about you, Racer?"*

Johnny kicked over the Philco highboy cabinet radio, silencing that son of a bitch Mitch Mills.

Rose stepped out of the kitchen. "Honey, is everything okay?"

Just then the ground and walls began to shake. A picture of him, Rose, and Dahlia fell off the wall.

Dahlia scurried down the stairs and rushed into her mother's arms. "Mom, what's going on?"

"It's an earthquake or tremor or something." Rose hugged Dahlia to shield her from the chandelier that started swaying.

"Johnny," Rose cried.

"Stay here. I'll handle this."

"Dad don't go."

"Don't worry, sweetie. Daddy will fix this."

Rose shuddered.

"It's the Syndicate." The darkness spoke in his head. *"They're the only force strong enough to interfere with the energy encapsulating this place."*

Why is the question.

Johnny marched out the door and was faced by the ever blue sky turned black as night.

All his dead neighbors hunkered down, scared. One peeked out the window at the chaos. "Johnny, you better get inside. This weather is dangerous," one neighbor called to him from the window.

Johnny waved him off and kept walking until he reached the neighborhood entrance. He stepped through the energy field preserving the space in time that was Remote Pines, and then he was suddenly standing on the dirt trail that led to the deserted road. Only the road wasn't empty this time. Hovering in the center was a shadowy black mass of a faceless man. From the black mass, tentacles made of dark energy stretched up and groped the fabric of Remote Pines. Every rattling and probing of the energy field made a corona discharge with a buzzing sound.

"Ah, Johnny Smith. There you are." A distorted voice emitted from the black mass. "I was wondering if you could hear me knocking. I'm the

Hat, the Boss sent me."

"You have my attention, but what happened to text messaging? A phone call? Email? I'm not that stuck in the past." Johnny held up his cellphone and then slid it back into his pocket.

"The Boss wanted to make sure you understood how seriously disappointed they are to hear the Dark Coast Racer is still alive and teaming up with the podcaster Mitch Mills." The mass all at once retracted the tentacles and formed arms and legs but still no face or color, just blacker than black, including the top-hat he wore.

"You heard about that already?" Johnny asked, surprised. "I just now got the word."

"Not much happens in the Dark Coast without the Syndicate knowing about it. You of all should know that, Assassin."

"I can assure you and the Syndicate that I killed the Racer the last time. And the time before that. Whoever it is, it's an imposter. As for the podcaster, he is a minor threat. He and his friend will be delt with accordingly. And whoever this imposter racer is too, if he's even real."

"This is your last chance, Johnny Smith." With an explosion of darkness, the Hat disappeared into a vortex of shadows that had opened behind him.

"He's a powerful entity," the voice said. *"We would not be a match."*

"We must kill the podcaster and whoever is helping him. That will make the Syndicate happy."

"What about the Racer?"

"The racer is dead. I'm not worried about an imposter."

Chapter 17

Mitch looked out the filthy window of his rundown home. *She should be here any moment.* Morgan Roth was the real person behind the name Beach Rat Queen. She had survived the Guild of the Beach Rats concert that was hit by a hurricane some time ago. He wasn't sure when she had started writing into the show, but it was sometime after the hurricane. Now she was a major contributor. Mitch had a feeling they'd meet one day, to collaborate on a much larger scale. This was that day. The occasion felt big, as big as a hurricane. As big as vampires and hellhounds.

He lugged his suitcase and the bare minimum sound equipment he needed to do an on-the-go podcast, guerilla warfare style. After he had loaded the trunk and back seat of his Mustang GT, he looked up to see the setting sun and an Uber driver dropping off a passenger. She looked younger than he'd expected...and blonde.

"Beach Rat Queen, it's good to finally meet you."

"You can call me Morgan. Big place you have

here."

"Thanks." Mitch watched her look the mansion over. She had a softer demeanor than her online presence. He was getting mouse vibes rather than the cunning fox he had hoped for. He'd noticed her choice of word for describing his *place*: big...but not *nice*. He knew the family estate was in shambles; he barely had enough money to keep the lights on much less pay for exterior upkeep. "Is that all you brought?" He indicated her backpack.

"I travel light."

He took it and pointed to his Mustang GT. "Your chariot awaits."

She followed him to the car. "How far is our rendezvous point?"

All business. I like it. "We're going about two hours away..." he stashed the backpack in the trunk, "but I'll get us there in one."

"Just get us there in one piece." Morgan climbed into the passenger seat.

Mitch got in and fired up the 5-liter Coyote engine. Tuned exhaust made her sound sweet. "I don't know about you, but I'm excited to meet the Dark Coast Racer at his shop."

#

One hour later, Mitch was on the highway into the industrial district of Dark Coast City. Morgan seemed reserved. He wasn't sure what to make of that.

She gripped the handhold over the door as he switched lanes. "Please slow down."

He glanced in the rearview mirror to see the same car that had been there since they'd left Dark Hills. He decided to tell her. "We're being followed."

"What?" She whipped around as if she didn't believe him. "Are you sure?"

"Could be the Slasher."

"It's not an old white luxury car."

Mitch noticed it was a sedan. "It could be stolen. Something he plans to ditch after he kills us."

"Paranoid much?"

"If you'd walked a mile in my shoes, you'd know why. I'm going to try to lose him."

Morgan gripped the handhold tighter.

He floored the gas, cut in front of a semi, and blasted down an exit ramp. The sedan remained steady on course. He scanned the rearview mirror and side mirrors. "Looks like I lost him."

"My hero," Morgan replied, but from her tone, she seemed unimpressed, or something else was bothering her. He wasn't used to being with her in person, so her crassness could well be normal.

He drove past a hotdog vendor on the corner and stopped in front of an open garage door. The

GPS announced they had arrived at I&R Customs.

"Thank God," Morgan blurted. She bailed out as if the car was on fire.

"My driving isn't that bad." He figured Morgan was extremely squeamish. He hadn't driven over a hundred miles an hour, and the only erratic maneuver was the lane-buster getting off the freeway. On this mission, squeamish could get her killed.

A mechanic in greasy coveralls stepped out of the garage. "You Mitch Mills?"

He shut off the Mustang and got out. "I am. Are you the Dark Coast Racer?"

He laughed. "I'm Isaac."

Mitch extended a hand to shake Isaac's. Beside him stood a young woman. Slim and trim, and with those long legs, she could have been mistaken for a runway model. He nodded to her. "Are you the Dark Coast Racer?"

She laughed.

Isaac took the question. "This is my friend Row. Isaac said her name with a hint of pride.

"Hi." Row waved.

Mitch motioned to Morgan standing behind the Mustang. "This is Beach Rat Queen, Morgan Roth. Our lead on the case."

She nodded and waved.

"I'm still trying to get her to break out of her

shell." He looked around, took in an ordinary auto shop with cars parked about, a couple greasy oil drums along the wall, a floor jack by the door. "So, where's the Racer?"

"He's coming. You find this place alright?"

"I think we were being followed. A sedan of some kind. I lost him."

Isaac frowned. "Then let's get inside."

Mitch looked back. Morgan was on her phone. "Come on."

When he walked inside, he quickly forgot about Morgan. There, in the first bay sat a legend. The Cuda. All black. Clean as the day she rolled off the assembly line in 1970. He circled the muscle car, ran his fingertips down the fender. They tingled as if tickled by static electricity. Being an investigative podcaster, he had to wonder if it was the real McCoy or a replica. It certainly looked like the car pictured in a tabloid he'd seen on the internet. "So, this is *the* Cuda?"

Isaac saw the skepticism in Mitch's hooded eyes. "The Dark Coast Racer modified it himself. I can assure you it's the real deal."

"Very slick."

"Hello, Mitch." The voice came from the radio.

He jumped back. "What's this? Some kind of David Hasselhoff Nightrider type-shit?"

"I talked with you earlier...on the podcast."

Row spoke up. "That's my brother, Ramon."

"So...Ramon? You're the Dark Coast Racer?"

"My dad was first. Ralph Murphy."

Mitch felt lightheaded, mesmerized by the phenomenon. The son of a dead legendary Racer talking to him from a car radio. A ghost?

Fascinating...

"Morgan. You getting this?" He looked at her standing behind him. She showed little interest in the car, the voice on the radio, in the supernatural implications playing out right in front of her. Let alone a car that had manifested itself into actual interacting matter. After all, it was she who had geeked out earlier. Was it a show? Mitch shrugged it off as a classic case of hero disappointment.

'Never meet your heroes.'

"Can we get down to business now?" Morgan asked. "When do we go in?"

Mitch tweaked a brow. Maybe she was interested, after all. "Right, we need to hammer out the details. Morgan and I will be at my sponsor's table, Dark Coast Brewery. They've agreed to let me broadcast my live stream from there. Granted, they know we've received death threats from Slasher."

Row asked, "Where do you want me and Uncle Isaac?"

"Uncle Isaac can't go in. He can't be seen."

Row frowned. "Wait, why?"

Isaac touched her shoulder. "Because the Slasher will recognize me from before. I can wait in the car with Ramon."

"Row, you'll go in undercover with us, but you have to be ready to get to the Cuda if the Slasher tries to get away."

"Alone?"

"I'll be with you," Ramon said through the speakers.

"Me, too," Isaac put in.

"Great. I feel better already."

"I can't be on the inside to cover her," Isaac said. "We need someone she trusts to go in with her."

"I'm on it." Row pulled out her cellphone and sent a text message.

Morgan jumped in. "How are you going to get the Slasher when he shows up? Call 911? Tackle him? What?"

Mitch shrugged. "Corner him. Apprehend him. Expose him for the devil that he his."

"Get real, you guys." Isaac leaned against the fender of the Cuda. "I've seen him in action. He can nail you with a throwing knife before you even know he's there. Look what he did to Ralph and Ramon. He's unstoppable."

"You stopped him," Ramon said from the radio.

"With your helmet, man. Any ordinary helmet would have shattered. Besides, it only slowed him down."

"Gave us time to get away."

"How did that work out for you, Ramon? You're dead."

The radio buzzed. "Then you'll have to kill the son of a bitch."

"Too risky," Mitch said. "There are going to be too many eyes at this event. Witnesses. Assuming he can be killed."

"He can die," Ramon said coldly through the speakers.

"Maybe." Mitch looked at the crew. Morgan was their weakest link, strangely, when he thought she'd be their greatest asset. However, as a reporter, she'd asked the right questions: *When do we go in? How do we get him?* She already knew the who and where of the story. Still, something wasn't right about her.

What am I missing?

Chapter 18

The iconic guitar-shaped tower erected in the middle of the casino complex was a 638-room luxury hotel. It resembled two electric guitars standing back-to-back, and the frets were lit up with neon lights. Moonlight and the city skyline reflected off the glass exterior of the tower, creating a surreal, psychedelic effect. Ground-based spotlights scattered throughout the complex swept the sky. The Dark Rock Hotel and Casino complex hosted several smaller casinos, a nightclub, a music hall, and a Greyhound racetrack.

To Row, it seemed like this event had attracted celebrities who turned out in their flashy attire. Stretched limousines lined the drive to the ritzy portico. She hadn't realized the combined gambling and racing event would draw so many people, but thousands were flocking in from the complex parking grounds. Shuttle busses bulled along, painted up like Dark Rock was a theme park. A country music star was booked to play, which made the event more attractive to the common folks.

"Damn, Miley Cyrus." Isaac spoke over the commlink in Row's ear. "I'd like to catch that show."

"Makes me wonder how the Slasher is going to make his move with so many people around." Row felt like a special agent speaking into the commlink without being noticed.

Mitch put in, "My Spidey-sense is tingling."

Row stood outside the Dark Rock Hotel and Casino, on the steps leading to the ground-floor entrance. She inhaled a deep breath, got as mentally ready as possible. Her presence turned heads and caught stares. Yeah. She was looking hot in this slinky red dress and matching heels. The slit up the side made her legs look longer. Still, she was modestly dressed compared to a lot of the other attendees: furs and funky hats; gowns and bowties. Sunglasses at night? A couple wore matching all-white ensembles: slacks, coattails, and top-hats. She felt like daffodil in a garden of roses.

At the first of the week, when she thought her life was ending in a lot of ways, she did not expect her path to go this direction. After signing her mother over to the mortuary and walking out of the hospital, she'd met the ghost of her brother in their father's notorious hotrod. Now she was the Dark Coast Racer. She didn't know what that title really meant: vigilante justice, revenge, thrills, but she knew the Assassin and her family had bad blood, something otherworldly, it seemed, a curse that spanned generations. *I could die trying to end this one.* She didn't want to die, but she knew it was the kind of attitude this mission required. *Do or die.*

I want to see Jeremy, but he couldn't know the truth. Not here. Not like this. It would be too dangerous.

Her phone vibrated. It was Jeremy. He had texted her. She wanted to see him, wanted his help, but he couldn't know the truth about the danger she would be facing.

"I'm here. Walking up."

And there he was, six feet tall with shaggy hair. He cleaned up well, though, with his bangs brushed to the side and tucked behind his ear. He wore a gray blazer and a fresh-out-of-the-pack black t-shirt. Row could tell by the crisp neckline. He ogled her like she'd stepped out of a dream.

"Eyes up here, Shaggy."

"You look great." He blushed and hugged her. His dimples were cute enough to pinch.

"I've never been to this place," Jeremy said, glancing around.

"Me either. Pretty cool, though."

"Stay sharp, kids," Isaac chimed in through the earpiece. "The Slasher can strike at any time."

Row ignored him as Mitch started his Podcast over the shared commlink. *"Welcome, Dwellers..."*

Jeremy said, "I didn't know you were such a fan of Dark Coast to Coast that you'd come to a live broadcasting."

"There's a lot we don't know about each other."

"Keep it moving," Isaac said. "Get a seat close to the vendor section."

"Come on, let's hurry. It's starting." Row took Jeremy by the hand and guided him through the doors of the Dark Rock Hotel and Casino.

Inside, the neon wheels and slots flashed in a spectacular display of wanton greed. The ceiling was decorated with music notes, and in another section of the casino, the ceiling shined of guitars and strings. Her red high heels started to hurt her feet, and she wished she had worn flats.

"We are here at the Dark Rock Hotel and Casino..."

They took a seat at a high-top table close enough to see Mitch and Morgan from where they were posted down vendor alley. They shared table space with their sponsor, Dark Coast Brewery. A woman with flowing hair, perfect makeup, and a Florida tan, gave out sipping cup samples of beer.

Morgan gave Row and Jeremy a discreet nod then nudged Mitch. He adjusted his headset and appeared not to pay them any attention.

A cocktail waitress checked their IDs. She ordered a vodka martini. Jeremy ordered a draw of light Dark Coast beer.

"This is quite the first date. Thanks for inviting me." He slid his arm across the table and gently touched her hand.

"You did say I owed you one date." She left out the part that this may be her last night on earth if the Slasher got his way. "Don't forget. You promised not to talk about our childhood."

"I know...so, how's Isaac? You two were close, right? You keep in touch?"

"Oh, boy," Isaac scoffed in her ear. "This guy is going all in. Don't let him distract you, Row."

"Isaac is same as usual, a jackass."

"I'm mortified," Isaac said.

The waitress brought their drinks. Jeremy ordered a basket of French fries for the table while Row turned her attention to Mitch Mills.

"I have my guest host beside me, Beach Rat Queen."

"Hi," Morgan said flatly.

"She's a bit microphone shy. We want to thank Dark Coast Brewery for hosting us this year. Distributing the refreshments is their very talented rep, Kimberly."

Kimberly, wearing a crop top and cut-off shorts, performed a professional cheerleader kick and hooted for the crowd.

Passersby gawked at Kimberly's cleavage and

shapely legs.

"Come by our table in the east wing, get a free sample of our famous Dark Coast stout, and meet Kimberly in person."

Row felt a tongue licking her ankle. She glanced at Jeremy sipping from his beer glass with one hand and drowning a French fry in ketchup with the other, totally oblivious as to what was going on around him. She glanced under the table to see a little dog licking her right ankle. It was a Maltese wearing a therapy dog vest. "What the hell?"

Jeremy looked down. "Aw, cute dog."

"It's slobbering all over my shoes."

"Samson," a woman said in a stern voice.

Samson stopped licking and ran toward the woman. She wore Converse shoes and an army jacket with a bandolier style purse strapped across her chest. Row thought she was trying to make doomsday prepper look stylish.

Samson jumped into the woman's arms. "Sorry about this little furball here. He likes you."

"He seems sweet." Row wiped her ankle with a table napkin, giving Jeremy a view not even Kimberly could match.

"Well, enjoy your evening. I'm going to go try a sample of the stout over there." She pointed to the Dark Coast table...and gasped. "Good heavens."

Row turned to see shadows under the table expand and rise in the shape of hands that snatched Mitch and Morgan and dragged them, kicking and screaming, into...what? A blackhole? And just as quickly, the shadows returned to normal. Kimberly fainted. It had happened so fast, people milling about clearly missed what had transpired.

"No way," Row yelled. "What was that?"

"I saved you some fries and ordered wings for the table." Jeremy hadn't noticed the disturbance in the shadows, either.

The woman ran away, staring at her phone, maybe calling 911. Samson was running at her heels.

Isaac shouted in her ear. "Row, what happened? What's going on in there?"

Row looked at Jeremy. She didn't know how to tell him that shit had hit the fan. "I gotta go."

"Wait. What?" Jeremy's eyebrows arched. "Was it something I said?"

"No...it's not you. It's me..." Row jumped up. "I'll text you later." She scrambled toward the Dark Coast Brewery table. Her heels did not make running easy. "Isaac. Slasher's got Mitch and Morgan."

"Find them, Row. Find them," Isaac shouted.

Chapter 19

Mitch plunged into blackness mid-sentence. It felt like a dark wave had washed over him...and Morgan, dragged them through the floor. He'd grabbed her hand. Now they were surrounded by shadows, and shadow ropes constricted around their bodies, tying them to the chairs they had been sitting in.

And then there was light.

Morgan squirmed in the chair next to him.

Mitch studied the situation. The podcast equipment was still linked up. He had been under the spell of shadow magic before, but this magic was not vampiric like in Bone Valley. Nevertheless, it remained restrictive, impeding circulation as he attempted to free himself.

He could see they were in a room in the glass guitar tower. The view was from somewhere near the top overlooking the casino complex.

"Hello, Mitch Mills and Morgan Roth."

The sudden deep and ethereal voice made his arm hairs stand on end. It came from a shadow in the corner. "Who's there?"

"I warned you to stop talking about me."

"The Slasher," Mitch stated and gulped.

"Now I'm going to gut you like a pig."

"Mitch. Where are you?" Isaac called over the commlink in his ear.

There were 638 rooms. He didn't know which one he was in. There was no way anyone would get here in time. They were doomed...unless...he could stall. Mitch couldn't out-right talk to his team, but he could give them clues as to where they were.

"Help," Morgan screamed.

"Save your breath." The Slasher stepped out of the shadows, revealing a youthful man wearing a suit from out of the 50s. Mitch had never seen a colder blue gaze. "The room is shielded in shadow magic." He rolled a gold coin across his knuckles, back and forth, a cheap parlor trick. "And the festivities below will drown out any screams, no matter how loud you scream."

"Looks like you've thought this one out, Slasher."

"Don't call me that." The Slasher brandished a knife, a really big knife.

Mitch about shit his pants. "Okay. Wait. How about Johnny? You are Johnny, right? Johnny Smith."

The Slasher put the blade to Mitch's throat. "You think you're so smart. You don't know the real

Johnny Smith. I've carved up smarter men than you. I killed the Dark Coast Racer...twice. Now you're next."

"I...I..." Mitch clenched his butt cheeks. He didn't want to be known as the podcaster who shit himself before he was murdered by the Dark Coast Slasher. "Okay. Okay. Hold on. How about, well, at least let me say farewell to my listeners."

The Slasher lowered his knife as if debating whether to grant the request.

Mitch took the opportunity. "Dwellers, there's been a turn of events here at Dark Rock. Morgan and I've been kidnapped. I must say, I didn't see this one coming. The Slasher used shadow magic to nab us. Sucked us right through the floor and teleported us to a room somewhere in the guitar tower. Possibly on the 35th or 36th floor."

"Keep talking," Row said through the commlink. "I'm heading toward the elevators now."

"Enough." The Slasher seemed to realize what Mitch was doing and snatched the headset from his head. The knife was raised again. "It's time to die, fool. And your little blonde friend is next."

Mitch squinted. *This is it. Dad, Jessica, Dean,* he thought of loved ones in Heaven. *I'll see you soon.*

"Wait," Morgan shouted. "I can't do this anymore. I'm not the real Morgan Roth." She started crying. "I don't want to die."

Mitch opened his eyes. He wasn't stabbed to death, yet. "What? I knew something was off with you." Mitch thought back on the moment she was dropped off at his address and all the oddball moments leading up to this point.

The Slasher was mid-swing but paused to hear the confession, then: "If you're not Morgan, who are you?"

"My name's Heather Hudson. I'm just an intern at Masque Media. Please don't kill me."

If Heather was here and she wasn't Morgan Roth, then where was the real Morgan Roth? By the look the Slasher was giving her, he had the same question. Just then, the door was busted open. A woman wearing Converse burst in, wielding a Glock and accompanied by a little Maltese dog.

Caught off guard, the Slasher spun around.

The little dog sprang into action, latching its jaws onto the Slasher's ankle. He screamed in anger and started shaking his leg back and forth, trying to fling the pesky dog loose. The woman opened fire. A bullet struck the Slasher in the thigh, and another grazed his shoulder and busted out the window behind him.

Glass rained down to the street below. *That'll get someone's attention.*

Johnny tossed the knife at the woman.

But she'd already ducked into the bathroom. The knife stuck in the doorframe.

The dog unlatched its jaws and chased after the woman, as if to check on her.

The Slasher turned toward the wall where the shadows were clumped together, forming a portal that he jumped into. Mitch noted it took longer for the shadows to respond to the Slasher, as though being hurt weakened his magic ability.

As the shadows dissipated, the room's lighting returned to normal. The shadow ropes that bound them to the chairs vaporized.

"Mitch," Isaac shouted through the commlink in Mitch's ear. He'd worn it under the headset. "What's going on? Did you get him?"

"Be on the lookout. The Slasher is on the move. He's wounded."

"Copy that," Isaac replied.

"Got it," Row chimed in. "I'm at the main elevators."

"Hello." A voice came from the bathroom. "Is it all clear?"

"Morgan," Heather shouted. She got up, crying, and rushed toward the bathroom.

Mitch picked up his headset and slammed it into position. "Dwellers, I've got a crazy twist to report. Some flea-flicker type trick play if I've ever seen it. The Slasher is wounded and on the run.

Morgan wasn't really Morgan, but the real Morgan Roth is with us now. We're taking a brief intermission." Mitch's heart was still racing. He took a deep breath.

"All clear," Mitch declared.

Heather and the woman Mitch now presumed was the real Morgan came out of the bathroom. The little dog trailed them.

"Morgan, I'm so sorry I buckled. I tried to keep my cover."

"It's fine, Heather. I don't blame you. The guy's a supernatural serial killer. You did good for your first undercover assignment." Morgan patted her back. "Your sister Blaire would have been proud."

"Ahem," Mitch made an annoyed noise.

"Mitch Mills. Nice to meet you, officially."

"Likewise. What an entrance."

"Sorry about keeping you in the dark."

"Are you kidding? It was brilliant. I'm guessing that was you tailing me when Heather and I first set out?"

"Yeah," Heather piped in. "I should've known you'd spot her."

"But the Slasher got away." Morgan scanned the room.

"Yeah, through a shadow portal. Too bad you're not a better shot."

"What does he look like?" Row asked into the commlink.

"A shadow. He's hobbling from a bullet in the leg. And he has the coldest blue eyes I have ever seen."

Chapter 20

Row hated leaving Jeremy in such a state of confusion. She glanced back at the table where he stared at her, stunned. Kimberly was mumbling incoherently in the middle of the floor. The crowd backed away as if she had the plague. Security guards pushed through the crowd from the other side of the vendor area.

"Mitch. Morgan. Come in," Isaac called over the commlink.

There was no response from them.

Kimberly cowered on the floor with her knees to her chest, rocking back and forth. "Shadows. Them. They. Were. Gone."

She would be of no use to anyone in her current state.

People took pictures and recorded her with their phones.

Despicable.

There was a tap on her shoulder. She turned to see Jeremy with the basket of fries in his hand. "I don't know what's going on. But can I help?" He said it with such sincerity. Row wanted to say yes, but instead she was distracted by hearing Mitch and the Slasher go back and forth over the commlink like a villain and hero in a B-grade movie.

Jeremey started speaking again, but as Mitch called out his final farewell to his listeners, her attention felt annihilated by all the commotion: people around her and the voices in her head, from Isaac, Mitch, the Slasher; she could hear it all through Mitch and Morgan's microphones.

The security guards were now tending to Kimberly and disbursing the crowd, which also drew her attention away from everything Jeremy was saying.

"....*We are now somewhere in the guitar tower. Possibly on the 35th or 36th floor.*"

"You mean a lot to me, Row. You have since we were kids."

"I..." *I can't do this now.* "I told you not to talk about our childhood." She pushed past him, knocking some French fries from the basket.

"Keep talking," Row said into the commlink. "I'm headed toward the elevators."

You mean a lot to me, Row, she thought while squeezing through the crowd. *What did he mean by that? Love? Marriage? Kids? A house with a white picket fence? It's his fantasy. Not mine.* She wondered if she'd ever get through to him how she felt about him digging up old memories. Right now, finding Mitch and Morgan before the Slasher killed them was more important than his obsessive nostalgia.

She stopped in the middle of the walkway.

Jeremy ran into her and dropped his fries. "Sorry."

She had turned toward the stairs and not the elevators. Her thoughts were scattered, concentration muddied on account of Jeremy's ill-timed romantic overtures.

Damn. When she had turned her compass correctly toward the elevators, she heard Morgan over the commlink. *"I'm not the real Morgan Roth."*

What?

"My name's Heather Hudson. I'm just an intern at Masque Media. I don't want to die."

What followed were sounds of a dog attack, the Slasher's angry scream, and gunshots. Row felt sick to her stomach, listening to the pandemonium. *All hell is breaking loose up there.* She made it to the elevators.

"Did you get him?" Isaac asked over the commlink.

"The Slasher is on the move. He's wounded."

"Copy that," Isaac replied.

"Got it. I'm at the elevators." Row pressed the button to go up. She had just missed one elevator that took a group of people who were waiting before her. She noticed an elevator on its way down and positioned herself in front of the door. "What does he look like?"

"A shadow. He's hobbling from a bullet in the leg. And he has the coldest blue eyes I have ever seen."

At that moment, the elevator doors opened, revealing a tall man with an ice-blue gaze. He hobbled as he shoved past her, seemed to not notice her standing there.

"I have eyes on him," she whispered. "He's on the ground floor." Row reversed course, but folks waiting for the elevator slowed her down. She damn near lost sight of him.

"Row, be careful," Isaac said.

She hung several paces behind the Slasher as he bulled through the crowd. At the main entrance, he shoved past a young couple, knocking them over as he made his escape. Security was still assisting the hysterical Kimberly.

"Hey, watch it, buddy," the guy yelled as he helped his date get up from the floor.

The Slasher didn't even look back.

Row kicked off her high heels. She knew she had no chance of keeping up with him unless she went barefoot.

In the parking lot, the Slasher hobbled between parked cars, mumbling to himself. Multiple lampposts cast his shadow in every direction. As the gambling tournament was in full swing, the parking lot was all but empty of people.

"Row, I can see you from here," Isaac said. *"We parked in the back near the dumpster area."*

"Someone is following me?" the slasher shouted. "Damn it." He seemed to be talking to a devil on his shoulder.

Row stopped and ducked behind a car just as the Slasher peered behind him. She stayed low and held her breath.

"Row, you're clear. He's back on the move."

She crab-walked to the front of the car, careful where she placed her bare feet, as the Slasher was leaving a trail of blood droplets toward the dumpsters.

Isaac spoke up. *"He's heading straight for us."*

She ventured a glance over a car hood. The Slasher lifted his hand and swiped the air. The motion revealed a classic white T-8 luxury car parked a hundred yards from the Cuda.

"Holy shit," Isaac said. *"He uses some kind of cloaking shadow magic."*

"Fascinating. Can you get pictures?" Mitch came through on the commlink.

The slasher wasted no time starting the engine. The car peeled off toward the exit.

Row hurried to the driver side of the Cuda and jumped in.

"He's getting away," Isaac shouted.

As Row gripped the steering wheel and the engine blasted on, her outfit materialized into the Racer's leathers, including the helmet and a pair of boots. "Buckle up." She floored the gas and took off after the Slasher.

"Careful, Row," Ramon warned.

"What's happening, guys?" Mitch came through on the commlink.

"We're in pursuit of the Slasher."

Row turned the wheel hard right to follow the path the Slasher took from the parking lot and onto the highway. The Cuda quickly gained on the classic car. It was driving straight toward a swirling vortex of shadows, a portal to oblivion, for all she knew.

"Where the hell did that come from?" Isaac shouted.

"What are you seeing?" Mitch demanded.

Row watched the black hole suck the Slasher's vehicle into the rift. She let off the gas, got ready to slam on the brakes. "Ramon. What should I do?"

The portal started shrinking.

"It's now or never." Ramon declared.

"This one is for you and dad." She gunned the throttle. The Cuda leaped to top speed in less than three seconds. The night went by in a blur. Either she'd reach the portal before it closed or the Slasher would get away.

From the corner of her eye, she saw Isaac pressed into the seat from the inertia of acceleration. His face morphed into some grotesque manifestation of himself.

The Cuda blasted through the portal just as it closed.

Swallowed by swirling blackness, the car tilted and rolled through a barrage of lightning flashes as if it had reached the warp speed of a futuristic spaceship. Bolts of energy reflected a swirl of purple and dark blue electrons flowing through a tunnel that appeared to stretch to infinity. Beyond the spiraling portal, shimmering particles appeared, bright white like distant stars of the galaxy. Row feared the Cuda had escaped terminal velocity and was now screaming into eternity. The end of the universe suddenly contracted. There was a spark, a flash, blackness, and then Row felt the car's wheels gain traction on a deserted road that came out of nowhere. The Cuda tore through the night, following the white luxury car's taillights.

Isaac patted his body as if to make sure all his pieces were still intact. "Where are we?"

The radio buzzed. "The middle of Florida," Ramon said. "Three hundred miles from the Dark Rock Hotel."

"What's way the hell out here?" Row saw the

old road was blocked by forest overgrowth. "It's a dead end."

The Cuda flashed by a weathered sign: *Remote Pines.*

"Holy shit," Isaac exclaimed. "The lost suburb."

The Cuda careened by a crumbling brick wall.

"Mitch, you copy?"

Nothing but static.

"We're too far away for a signal."

Row let off the gas.

The Slasher's classic car disappeared into the brush.

"It's an illusion." Ramon spoke over the radio. "Drive through it."

Row trusted her brother, but glanced over to Isaac.

He gave her a nod of reassurance. "Let's take the bastard out for good." He held up a tire iron like he was wielding Thor's Hammer.

"What do you think you're going to do with that?"

"Knock him into next Tuesday. Got it out of the trunk while you were inside. Best weapon I could come up with on short notice."

Row liked his confidence but didn't have time to explain the error in his thinking, as the Cuda busted through an energy field encapsulating

Remote Pines. Instantly it went from night to daylight. The Slasher had parked his classic car at the entrance to an unfinished suburban haven. Six large houses with matching yards and driveways lined the roadside.

She slammed on the brakes. "I don't see him." She twisted frantically in her seat to check the area beyond each window.

"Row, there." Isaac pointed to her side window where the Slasher had suddenly appeared. His face was an ancient mask of rage. He pulled the door open and grabbed Row's arm. She held onto the wheel, but she lost her grip as he yanked out of the driver's seat. He shoved her against the Cuda, held a knife drawn to her throat.

She couldn't breathe. She couldn't scream. She could only look death in the face.

"No...not yet. I want to know..." The Slasher was talking to himself. "I need to know." He pressed the blade to the skin under her helmet, drawing a thin line of blood. "Who are you?"

Row's heart thundered in her chest. She used both hands on his wrists, hoping to keep the knife from cutting any deeper.

"There's no way you're not dead. Answer me. Who are you?"

In came Isaac with the tire iron, holding it with both hands. *Batter up!* "Remember me?" He swung and hit the Slasher over the head.

He stumbled and fell, tried to get up, but Isaac was on him, locked and loaded for another swing of the tire iron.

A blade slid out of the Slashers coat sleeve and blocked the blow. With an upward kick to the stomach, the Slasher sent Isaac flying backwards. He hit the fender of the Cuda and fought to catch a breath.

The Slasher pushed himself back up to his feet and charged Isaac with the wrist blade.

"Wait," Row shouted. "You want to know who I am?"

He stopped his attack on Isaac and turned to her, clearly intrigued. "A woman?"

She pulled off her helmet and let her hair flow out.

The Slasher looked surprised, staring confused.

Isaac regained enough wind to launch himself the Slasher again. The tire iron found purchase on the side of his head. The blow sent him hurtling to the ground, where he moaned and started to crawl away from them.

Residents stepped from their homes and slowly walked toward the commotion at the end of the block. There, they stopped and gathered to look on in horror.

"Good heavens, Johnny," someone barked from the group. "What's the meaning of this?"

"Daddy?" a little girl yelled. Her mother held her close and stared at him lying on the ground, mortified.

"Go. Don't look. Go back to your houses," the Slasher yelled at them as he struggled back to his feet. "You don't want to see what I'm going to do to them." He was a bloody mess. His head was streaming blood from two run-ins with the tire iron, and he fought to stand straight, as gunshot wounds to his leg and shoulder painfully reminded him that he wasn't immortal, but a slave to the gold coin's black shadow magic.

"Johnny?" the woman holding the child cried out.

"Rose."

Row and Isaac watched the scene unfold, clinging to each other as if that alone would protect them from the tempest.

"Open the hood, Row, and get back," Ramon's voice commanded through the speakers.

She hurried to the Cuda's hood and unlatched the latch. The hood flew up, and she saw the faces of spiritual energy swirl within and roar like a V-8 Hemi. Remote Pines started to rumble and shake. She grabbed Isaac and pulled him back with her.

"What's happening?" Isaac shouted.

"I don't know."

The sunny blue sky started to peel away like shredded sheets of paper, revealing the real night sky behind it. Remote Pines' fabric of illusion was being ripped and torn apart and consumed by the Cuda's power.

Bit by bit, the town was broken down to expose its true form under the false fantasy. The pond dried up. Yards withered. Driveways cracked. The houses crumbled and turned hollow.

The particles and spiritual matter that made up the false reality shimmered and swirled through the air, only to be rapidly vacuumed under the hood. The last to be disintegrated into their true forms were the townspeople; their clothing dissolved to dust, revealing kill wounds where their throats had been slashed and their stomachs gutted. Their flesh rotted to bones, then dust, and then wailing ghosts joined those in the swirling energy under the hood.

"Daddy, I don't want to go."

"Johnny, why did you kill us?"

"Dahlia, Rose. I had to. It was the only way to keep us together forever."

"Our forever in nevermore, Johnny." The Slasher's wife and child reached out to him before turning into phantoms as the vortex sucked them into the Cuda's engine compartment.

The particles funneled together into a beam of light that pierced the Slasher's chest. The power under the hood drew him in. "No!"

Row rushed to close the hood. The Slasher's decaying hand grabbed her wrist. She saw him clinging to the underside of the hood; his feet dangled over the ethereal swirl. The hands of his daughter and wife and the others Johnny had killed groped and clawed upward at his feet to pull him down with them.

"Help me," the Slasher yelled.

"You killed my dad, *and* my brother... Burn in hell."

His eyes went wide at the realization of who she really was. "You. You're the Dark Coast Racer now." He grinned. "And I'll take you to hell with me."

With a panicked tug, she tried to take back her wrist. "Let me go." His grip was too strong. She was doomed.

Isaac rushed in with the Racer's helmet and bashed the Slasher in the face, knocking him unconscious. He released her wrist and the hood and fell into the arms of eternity. A gold coin flipped up from the swirling mass of misery and tumbled back down to be with Johnny Smith forever.

She slammed the hood and fell back on her

butt with a huff.

"You, okay?" Isaac extended his hand for her to grab.

She stood with his help, and they hugged under a starry night sky. "I thought we were goners, Uncle Isaac."

"Nah, no way the universe was going to let him kill us."

They released their heartfelt embrace.

He handed her the helmet, bloody but not much worse for wear and tear. "You're going to need this to drive us home."

She looked it over, wiped a smudge off on her pant leg. "Why did you hit him with this and not the tire iron?"

"It wasn't much help. He kept getting back up. That helmet has supernatural powers."

"Thanks for saving me."

"I wish I could have saved your brother back then."

"He'll always be with us, you know."

"Yeah. Wait until Mitch and Morgan get a load of this place." Isaac looked around at the dark ruins of Remote Pines. "What about that new boyfriend of yours?"

"He's not my boyfriend."

"You should text him, tell him you're alright."

She got busy pulling out her cell phone and

responding to Jeremy's last text: *"WTF?"*

"Meet me where we used to catch the bus to school. Tomorrow, 8:00. I'll explain everything then." She slid her phone back in her pocket. "Let's go home."

"Row..." Ramon spoke up over the radio. "You've got a three-hundred-mile trip ahead of you, but this is where I get off."

Row gasped. "Ramon? What are you talking about? Of course you're going with us."

"We've rid the world of the Slasher. Now I have to go back."

"No! What about the Syndicate? They're still in business. You're not done yet."

"That's a fight for another time. You're on your own, sis. Isaac, keep the Cuda at the shop."

"Sure thing, Ramon. Safe travels."

"I love you guys." The radio buzzed and went silent.

"Ramon," she cried.

"He's gone." Isaac looped an arm around her shoulders.

"But not forgotten." She fought back a tear.

"His legacy is now yours."

Gritting her teeth, Row pulled on the helmet. "Then let's get to it."

"That's the spirit," Isaac cheered. "The Dark Coast Racer rides again."

Chapter 21

In the office at I&R Customs, Isaac sat back in his chair with his feet up on the desk, munching on a chilidog and watching the evening news on the flat screen TV mounted on the wall. He had been waiting for the story all day.

A suit-clad newscaster held a mike as he stood before the remnants of a dilapidated neighborhood. "Dark Coast News Reporting. Thank you for joining us. We are here with Morgan Roth, investigative reporter and owner of Masque Media. She's going to fill us in on the groundbreaking story of Remote Pines. Many Dark Coast residents are familiar with the legend of the suburb that vanished decades ago. It was thought that a sink-hole had swallowed it, though no evidence was ever presented." He turned to Morgan. She wore her trademark camo Army jacket and bandolero purse strapped across her chest. "Can you tell us what happened here the other night?"

"Row, get in here," Isaac shouted.

She didn't answer.

"Row. You're going to miss it. The bit about

Remote Pines is on the air. Morgan's on TV."

Still silence from the shop.

He chucked the last of his chilidog, washed it down with a swig of Mountain Dew, swung his feet to the floor, and rushed out to see what the hell was keeping her. He got to the doorway and realized the shop was empty.

The Cuda was gone.

#

As the sun set on the Dark Coast, Row gunned the Cuda toward the old bus stop to meet up with Jeremy. She owed him an explanation for running out on him at the casino. From her, he wanted more, she was sure by the things he'd said, though he was vague about what he meant. She could see now, that asking for his help and calling it a first date was a mistake on her part. For that she owed him an apology.

The V-8 Hemi purred as if the car knew better than to draw attention to itself with ear-splitting thunder and squealing tires. That stunt she'd pulled, smashing up the car club's rides, most likely put the Cuda on the BOLO list of every precinct in Florida. Still, that night, that act of revenge, had put her on a path she could have never foreseen. It was the turning point, the beginning, and like an eagle drawn to its nest, she felt the pull, the need to return to the place were it all began.

The last turn into the parking lot brought with it a disturbing sense of dread. Gavin and his crew had gathered under the lights to drink beer and act like fools. Loud music drowned out the rumble of the Cuda's engine. She idled it into the shadows, killed the engine, and turned off the headlights. Déjà vu made her hair follicles tingle under the helmet. The only thing missing was Ramon's voice in the radio. A tear burned in her eye. "Ramon. If you can hear me, what the hell am I doing here?"

She noted Gavin's Lancer still looked like it had survived a demolition derby. A new girl hung on his harm. Lucy must've seen him for the abuser he was, left him to pursue a Cosmetology career, or the new girl was a fling behind Lucy's back. Once a cheater, always a cheater. Once a beater, always a beater.

God, had I not seen Gavin's true nature, that could be me hanging on his arm, clueless to the danger and the heartbreak to come.

She ran her gloved fingers over the steering wheel and looked to the radio, its display dimly lit. "Now I know why I'm here, Ramon. To see my past, where I came from, the riffraff I called my friends...but where am I going from here?" She wished her brother's voice would answer her, or her dad's voice, any voice of reason, even her mom's.

"Ramon. You told me I'm not alone...but what do you call this? I am alone...well...accept for Uncle Isaac...but he isn't even my real uncle. I don't have any family left... You lied to me, Ramon. I am alone...and for what? That fight for another time? Me against the Syndicate? Who am I to take down a criminal enterprise that's plagued the Dark Coast for a hundred years?"

The radio remained mute, not even a buzz of static, a chirp of acknowledgement. Nothing.

"So that's your answer? I'm right? I'm alone and I have to be okay with it?" The display went dark. The Racer helmet felt suddenly heavy. Claustrophobic. A burden thrust upon her by a Hemi-powered legacy.

But I don't have to be alone. There's still Jeremy. He wants to be with me.

She fired up the engine, loped out to the street, and turned on the headlights. That electric feeling surged through her leathers, her gloves, the steering wheel, as if the car felt her pain, her conflicting emotions and wanted to sooth her, reassure her that the night road was where she belonged. Where vigilante justice ruled between the white lines, under the stars...and she finally got the message. *This is a road best traveled alone.*

She steered the Cuda around the corner onto the street where Jeremy and she had walked to catch the bus...when they were kids...innocent, and ignorant of the struggles life had in store. A Barbie doll, a Ken doll, a plastic convertible, all stepping stones into the real world...for her and Jeremy.

He was standing out by the stoop near the road. At the same spot all the neighborhood kids gathered to wait for the bus.

She glided the Cuda to a stop at the curb in front of him and rolled down the passenger window.

Jeremy stooped to look inside. "Can...ah..." His face turned pale under that mop of shaggy hair. "You looking for somebody, mister?"

She flipped up her visor.

"Row? What the hell?"

"Don't look so surprised to see me."

"What are you doing in this car...what's with the helmet...and the leathers? Are you kidding me?"

"I told you I'd meet you here. Get in."

He climbed in, futzed with the seat belt.

"Never mind that."

"Ah...Row...I don't know what to say."

"Just listen. I'm sorry about bailing on you at the casino."

"I had to thumb a ride home, Row. Sorry isn't enough. I want to know why."

"You wouldn't believe me if I told you. The

point is, I used you to get inside. I played on your feelings for me, our childhood, so I could get close to the Syndicate's assassin, their hitman...I put you in danger, and for that I apologize more than simply for the way I ditched you."

He wrung his hands in his lap, stared out the windshield.

"Jeremy, you don't have to forgive me."

"Remember when we were kids? We played Barbie and Ken. I really wanted to be your Ken." He looked at her. "But you don't want to be my Barbie, do you."

"Do you see this car? It's not Barbie's convertible. It's the Dark Coast Racer's car."

He shook his shaggy hair. "The legendary Dark Coast Racer? For real?"

"I'm all grown up, Jeremy. I don't want to look back. My path is set, and I must travel it alone."

"So no second date?" He grumped.

"No, Jeremy."

"Oh, so this was just an apology show. You could have texted me."

"A text would not have been believable. You needed to see this for yourself. This car. Me driving it."

"Well, that's all fine and dandy, Row. I believe it. And you need to believe this. You just broke my heart. Are you going to apologize for that too?"

"I won't apologize for being honest with you."

The passenger door popped open. "Good bye, Jeremy. I hope you find the love you deserve." She flipped down the visor.

"Good luck, Row. But like it or not, I'll always love you." He got out, closed the door, and stood at the curb with his hands in his pockets. To anyone who didn't know him, he could have been just any man standing alone on the street. Lonely. Broken. Defeated. But she knew he was a better man than most, just not the man for her.

With that, she rolled up the window, floored the gas, and sped off into the Dark Coast night.

More Books from Michael J.P. Whitmer

Guild of the Beach Rats

Morgan Roth, a defamed NYC journalist, returns to her Dark Coast hometown and finds it's been overrun by a snake-eyed cult. Nonconformists are hunted down, kidnapped, and converted. The Beach Rats, a ragtag bunch of kids, teens, surfers, and rebels refuse to heel to the cultist's demands. Their ancient deity, *Guabancex*, the Mother of Storms, sends Her wrath against the town. Max, a dead rock musician and Morgan's true love, is reanimated by the Master of the Guild to free the town and bring music back to the beaches.

Tales from the Dark Coast

Welcome to the Dark Coast of Florida.. Take a dangerous journey through the realms of the surreal and macabre, somewhere between the twisted regions of history and superstition, where imagination keeps pace with the moon, days become perpetual night, and neither offer comfort or peace. It's the frontline where the forces of good and evil clash at the shadowy edge of the inexplicable. Here, far beyond the utterly weird and supernatural, the human bonds of love and spirit will be tested in these three short stories from the twisted mind of Michael J.P. Whitmer.

Michael J.P. Whitmer

Bone Valley Vampires

Sebastian, a seminary school dropout, returns to his hometown of Dark Hills, Florida, to find his estranged brother, Elijah, who is obsessed with blaming the prominent Meszaros family for the murder of his parents, seven years prior. He claims they are vampires, but his quest for proof leads him down a dark path from which there is no salvation. Sebastian had given his grief to God, but his faith is put to the test as he and Elijah's allies are hunted by biker-ghouls and shadow creatures, spawns of the Bone Valley Vampires, bent on protecting their bloodthirsty lifestyle. Orchestrating the murder and mayhem, an ancient evil lies entombed in the phosphate bed beneath a reclaimed open-pit mine, plotting its resurrection to again enslave humanity for its blood sustenance. The brothers, once torn apart by grief, are now bound by opposing light and dark forces to do battle against the vampire god, Neferkare, and save the world.

Michael J.P. Whitmer is a speculative fiction/horror writer living in his sunny hometown of Jacksonville Beach, FL. He won the Watty Awards Best in Horror 2010 for his story "Day of the Undead Sophomores" and 2016 Theme of Absence's Halloween Horror Fiction contest for "The Girl in the Window." His other fiction has been released throughout the web and can be found in print anthologies UnCommon Lands, See Through My Eyes, and First Came Fear. Published by TWB Press in 2022, his "Guild of the Beach Rats" is another Dark Coast inspired tome, as are the "Bone Valley Vampires" and the three short stories in "Tales from the Dark Coast."

Michael J.P. Whitmer

Enjoy more short stories and novels by many talented authors at

https://www.twbpress.com

Science Fiction, Supernatural, Horror, Thrillers, Romance, and more